Roll Over, Big Toben

by

Victor M. Sandoval

PIÑATA BOOKS
ARTE PÚBLICO PRESS
HOUSTON, TEXAS

To my mother, who taught me perseverance.
For LuAnn, my inspiration.

This volume is made possible through grants from the City of Houston through The Cultural Arts Council of Houston, Harris County.

Piñata Books are full of surprises!

Arte Público Press
University of Houston
452 Cullen Performace Hall
Houston, Texas 77204-2004

Cover illustration and design by Lamberto Alvarez

Sandoval, Victor M., 1945–
   Roll Over, Big Toben / Victor M. Sandoval.
     p.   cm.
   Summary: Fifteen-year-old David López loses his father, his pigeons, and the leader of the gang in his Los Angeles neighborhood before he realizes that he must make an important choice for his future.
   ISBN 1-55885-401-0 (alk. paper)
   [1. Coming of age—Fiction. 2. Mexican Americans—Fiction. 3. Family life—California—Fiction. 4. Gangs—Fiction. 5. California—History—1950—Fiction.]   I. Title.
PZ7.S2187Ro 2003
[Fic]—dc21   2003049846
                                            CIP

∞ The paper used in this publication meets the requirements of the American National Standard for Information Sciences—Permanence of Paper for Printed Library Materials, ANSI Z39.48-1984.

3 4 5 6 7 8 9 0 1 2   10 9 8 7 6 5 4 3 2 1

CHAPTER 1

"**W**hy don't they all go away. I don't want them here," I said, my eyes still swollen nearly closed as I sat in my backyard with my best friend Robert.

"What happened in there, David?" Robert nodded his head toward the house and combed his fingers through his coarse black hair.

"It's my Uncle Joe," I replied, rubbing my index finger against a tiny scar that was half-hidden beneath my left eyebrow. "He's trying to tell me what I should and what I shouldn't do. Now that my father is . . . has . . . isn't here, my Uncle Joe thinks he can make all the decisions in my life. But he can't. It's not right. I won't let him." I leaned my right shoulder on the pigeon coop that stood against the six-foot-high cinder block wall that enclosed the yard. Looking through the wire mesh of the coop, I watched the birds. Several brown and white speckled pigeons cooed as they waddled. A large white one danced in a tight circle, showing off its fan of leg feathers. I took off my dark suit coat and rolled the sleeves of my white dress shirt up to my elbows. "I wish everyone would just go away."

"Does that go for me, too?" Robert asked.

"No, Robert, not you." I couldn't look up, but I reached

out and held onto Robert's shoulder. "It's just . . . I don't know . . . everything."

It was the morning of my father's funeral. I had awakened to the warm, sweet smell of *pan dulce* and *pan de huevo*. I remembered how my father would handpick them, using large metal tongs and a tray, selecting from the bread-cooling racks. From my room, I heard my mother in the kitchen preparing *carnitas*, *barbacoa de cabeza*, flour and corn tortillas. These familiar sounds and smells filled the house, a reminder of the fun and laughter that family gatherings brought. At those gatherings, my sister and brother would use the clean, white jaw bones of the calf's head as toy guns in a game of cowboys and Indians. And all day, there was plenty of *menudo*, my father's favorite tripe stew. He used to take a cooking pot to the Azteca Restaurant and get enough for friends and family. Today, after the funeral, only sad, grieving relatives and friends came to his house and to share his food.

"What did your Uncle Joe say that made you so mad?" Robert asked, rubbing the bridge of his nose with the knuckle of his finger.

"Oh, he warned . . . really ordered me to stay in school, go to college, stay away from the bad crowd . . . gangs," I paused. "And keep healthy, he says, don't play football at the park." I pounded my fist into my hand. "Who does he think he is?"

Robert shrugged his broad shoulders.

"He wants to pick my friends, plan my future, and keep

me from playing football. Even my father wouldn't . . . didn't do that."

"Maybe he's just trying . . ." Robert stopped, then started again. "Maybe he thinks you need someone now to . . ."

"No. My dad always let me make my own decisions. He never told me what to do. He let me decide, have the final say, but . . . now he's gone."

I turned and slowly opened one of the small, wire-mesh doors of the pigeon coop where a couple of tri-colored breeders huddled.

"My Uncle Joe wants me to sell the pigeons . . . all of them, the kips, breeders, and rollers." I began to cry. "My dad always said the pigeons could teach me a lot, if I just watched and listened to them."

I reached out and smoothed the breast feathers of the nearest cooing pigeon.

"Will you sell them?" Robert squeezed his eyes as though he regretted that he had asked.

Earlier my uncles, my father's brothers, had stood huddled together in a corner of the living room like strangers getting to know each other. Uncle Julio was a large man with a leather belt cinched at his waist by an extra hole he had punched in with a nail. He walked with a limp from a wound he got in the Korean War. Uncle Tomás, his head tilted up to meet the eyes of his older brothers, was short, but powerfully built with well-developed muscles and a poison wit. Uncle Joe, the oldest, never made a sound beyond an occasional grunt and sometimes a loud whistle to get a person's attention. El Cuate, Uncle Ricardo, whom everyone called Rico, was standing apart and talking to no one in particular.

"*Válgame Dios.*" Uncle Julio crimped my nose with his knuckles when I walked by. "Hey, you *mocoso*. You've grown quite a bit since I last saw you. How old are you now, *m'ijo?*"

"Just turned fifteen," I answered.

Then Uncle Joe gave a short whistle and motioned for me to meet and talk with him in the back bedroom. While I stared ahead into nothing, Uncle Joe told me what he would do if he were me. Finally, when Uncle Joe ended with a short grunt, I said nothing, left the room and went outside.

"They were my father's. The pigeons were special to him. I'll keep them as long as I can." My voice was low and faint.

"What do you mean by that?" Robert asked. "As long as you can?"

"I'm gonna split," I said. "I've got to get out of here."

"Run away?" Robert asked. "Where to . . . when?"

"I don't know yet, but I'm going to do it." I stared into

Robert's eyes, hoping he'd say something, anything.

"Hey, do me a favor?" Robert spoke softly. "Don't do anything . . . Don't split without telling me first?"

"Yeah, sure," I answered, turning once again to the pigeons. "But you know I can't do anything for a while anyway. My family needs me right now."

"Yeah, that's right." Robert's voice seemed to grow hopeful. "And the gang. You can't just take off like that."

I could see what Robert was doing. He understood that loyalty was a strong chain, binding me to my family and to my gang. I felt I did owe them something, but at this time of sadness, I didn't know what. All I knew was that I need-ed something to replace the black, spinning flood of empti-ness that was sucking me under like a bathtub drain. I felt Robert, though he seemed nervous and unsure, was throw-ing me a lifeline.

"You're right," I said. "I've got to stay, at least until . . ."

"Yeah, you've gotta stay." Robert appeared relieved as he put his arm around my shoulders. "We're the trouble-some twosome, remember? You have to stick around to fol-low through with all the hellraising we got planned to do at school this year. And the football games . . ."

"Hey, wait a second, Robert," I cut in. "I'm only stay-ing long enough to figure out what I need to do. You know what I mean?"

"Yeah . . . yeah, sure," Robert replied.

I didn't believe Robert. I knew even I, myself, didn't understand. I wanted to learn as quickly as possible what I needed to know before it was too late. Too late for what?

I didn't know.

I only knew that I felt a full-hungering emptiness of a missing part that hurt me in a scary new way—a sharp, cold, dark blade of pain I had never known until now.

CHAPTER 2

"Dedicated to the one I love"
—The Shirelles

Near the back of the bus the neighborhood girls were standing, singing the chorus of a popular tune, "This is dedicated to the one I love." Lucy, Anita, and Rachel were back-up, harmonizing, while Esther was belting out the words in high-pitched tones and heartfelt emotion. They were all rhythmically nodding their beehive hairdos cemented on their heads with hair spray and tons of hairpins, and swaying their bodies clothed in matching tight sweaters and skirts, which gave them the look of a main act on the *Ed Sullivan Show*.

When Esther cooed her last tone, we burst into loud applause. The bus driver smiled into his rearview mirror as she bowed proudly for her audience. This scene was repeated every morning, the song changing to whatever new tune was currently a top-ten hit on the radio. Most of the riders were high school students who traveled on the bus ten miles to Roosevelt High School, stopping only long enough to drop me and my friends at Wilson Junior High along the way.

Seated halfway down the aisle my friends and I grew restless as the bus bumped along to school.

"Poor Ricky want his booky?" I teased between short spurts of laughter.

"Sit down back there," boomed the school bus driver, when he saw that the playing around got rougher.

"He's got my book," yelled a seventh grader, pointing his finger at me.

"I said sit down!" The tall, angry driver tugged hard at the heels of his black leather gloves, as he waited for the red light to change.

"Hey, he's got my book. Give me my book!" the boy yelled and pointed.

"Yeah, give him his book," jeered the rest of the students, willing to add to the noise and fuss. They began to wave and snatch at the book that I held stretched above my head.

"Knock it off back there! Knock it off!" the bus driver yelled helplessly as he eased off the clutch. The bus jerkily rolled forward at the green light.

The brawl grew louder as Robert and I bent over the backs of our seats and banded together in a tug-of-war with the seventh grader over the book. Esther used her thick history book to keep a fat boy from leaning over her seat as he cheered on the others in front of him. I saw that most of the other girls remained calm and pretended not to be enjoying the noisy wrestling between the boys.

"All right!" the driver shouted as he slammed his foot on the brake, bringing the bus to a screeching halt. He jumped out of his seat and came down the aisle toward the racket, tugging at his gloves over and over again. Robert, the others, and I tumbled to the floor. Then we watched the driver get closer and closer.

"Okay, you, you, and you, get off." The bus driver pointed to us like a referee throwing players out of the game.

"Hey, I didn't do anything," I groaned.

"Shut up and get the hell off my bus—NOW!"

"All right, all right," I said as we stood up and made our way to the front.

"Come on, move it," the bus driver shouted. "And you, Esther, the one with the book, you get off, too."

Esther tossed her head and fingered the spit curls at her cheek. Then she strutted down the aisle to the exit.

As we filed down the aisle, we hooted and smiled at the on-lookers like TV wrestlers heading for the dressing room.

The driver followed us to the mechanical door and showed us out. Huddled on the curb, we pretended to be clown-sad and sorry. As he leaned out toward us from the steps of the bus, he announced: "And I don't want to catch any of you on my bus again. You'll have to walk the rest of the semester."

"That's not fair," I cried out.

"You heard me, stay off my bus, all of you!" He tugged

at his gloves with all of his strength as I watched him through the open doorway. Now standing next to his seat, the driver gave barbed-wire stares at the silent but expectant faces. Then he turned and sat down on a peeled banana one of the boys had placed on his seat when the driver wasn't looking. Outside, we all laughed as we ran, peeling off in all directions like birds let out of a cage.

Several blocks down the street, Robert and I sat resting on the curb. Robert was shorter than I was, but had muscles like his father.

"Wow, that was a riot," said Robert, grinning between breaths.

"Yeah," I gazed up at a covey of pigeons in the distance.

"We're going to be late for school again." Robert looked away.

"Yeah. Hey, Robert, look at those pigeons."

"Where?"

"Up there." I pointed. The high-flying white, beige, gray, and black pigeons seemed carefree.

"Oh yeah, I see them. Are any of them yours?"

"I think so. Watch them. They're called rollers. They'll close their wings in mid-air and let themselves drop and roll toward the ground like spinning tops. Then, at the last minute, only about thirty feet from the ground, they'll open their wings and ride the draft of warm air back up. See?"

Dark specks against the pale-blue sky, the pigeons seemed to be waiting in line at the lip of an updraft as I watched. The first one would fold its wings and legs tightly to its body and drop like a rock from a cliff. Then, a ruffled ball of feathers, the pigeon spread its wings like sails and floated up again, taking its place at the end of the line of flying birds. The circle of birds waiting, falling, and floating back up, continued for a long time. It seemed to me that their actions were carefree, but neat, like little kids taking turns on a playground slide.

"They're really getting a kick out of that, you can tell," I said, but then it hit me; I really hadn't talked about the pigeons with anyone, except Dad.

"Yeah. Did you see that? That brown one almost forgot to open its wings," Robert said, staring at the sky.

"It might be a suicide."

"A what?"

"A suicide pigeon. They're called that because some roller pigeons don't open their wings in time. They just hit the ground—WHAM!" I clapped my hands together.

"What?"

"Some of them spin so fast when they're falling that they black out."

"Wow!" Robert looked up with added excitement. "Hey, there's that brown one again."

We stared at the falling bird as it fell like a spinning lead weight, feathers a flutter.

"It's not going to open up!"

A second later the unconscious pigeon banged into the hood of a parked car. A loud, tinny thud brought us to our feet and, without even speaking, we raced toward the bird.

"It's dead. Its neck's broken," I said recognizing my bird as I climbed the bumper and leaned over the hood where the dead pigeon lay. I stared at the feathery body and its bloody beak. Then, picking it up carefully with both hands, I brought it to my chest. Its head fell between my thumb and forefinger like a pocket watch from a chain, showing the pink of its skin beneath the spreading fan of neck feathers.

"Hey, you kids, get away from my car," yelled a woman wearing pink foam hair curlers and a pink chenille bathrobe. She let the screen door slam as she stomped out the doorway toward us. "What are you doing? Do you hear me? Get away from my car! Why aren't you in school? Are you the bad boys that have been trampling my roses? Are you? What are you doing? What do you have there, any-way? My God! Killing birds! You terrible, terrible boys. Is that you, David? I'm calling the police. Killing birds, my God!"

"Let's get outta here."

We ran back to the curb where we had left our books and bag lunches and sat down.

"What are we going to do with it?" asked Robert, point-ing to the dead pigeon in my hand.

"Bury it, I guess."

"Where?"

"My backyard."

"But we can't go there now."

"Yeah, I know."

Sitting on the curb, I looked straight into the gutter water.

"Hey, ditching?" a voice from behind us called out.

Before I turned around, I slipped the pigeon into my lunch bag as Robert stood up and turned to face the voice. It was Big Toben.

"What are you guys doing?" demanded Big Toben, standing several feet away with his friend Speedo. Big Toben stared us down; his smooth round face was bordered by black wavy hair. I knew his rounded shoulders and slight bulge around his middle gave no hint of the brutal strength that was neighborhood legend. His real name was Danny. A few years earlier he had gotten his nickname, Big Toben, from a popular 1956 Chuck Berry song called "Roll Over, Beethoven," which, after awhile, sounded like "Big Toben," especially if you never read the record label.

"Waiting for the bus," answered Robert.

"Sure you are, man," said Big Toben, taking his hands out of his khakis. "The bus went by here a long time ago."

I held tightly to the bag at my side.

"Hey, look Speedo, they got lunches. Ya hungry?"

"I'm always hungry," Speedo answered right away.

"Gimme that lunch bag." Big Toben locked his eyebrows together.

"No," I said without thinking.

"Gimme it." Big Toben jumped at me, knocking me to the ground as he pulled the bag away. "Now get out of here, both of you."

Robert and I picked up our books and ran. I looked back long enough to see Big Toben, teeth shining, reach into the brown bag only to let it drop to the ground like a dirty diaper.

"Go get em', Speedo!" ordered Big Toben.

Looking over my shoulder as I ran, I could see Speedo gaining on us as we turned the corner for home.

"Split up, split up!" yelled Robert. When we reached the corner he went to the right and I went to the left.

With his long legs stretching like bubble gum, Speedo chased me as I leapt over low hedges, circled trees and headed for a backyard fence to climb. Just then, right in front of me, was Tía Cucuy. The crazy old woman wearing a black shawl down to the ground threw a handful of rose petals at me. She did this to everyone who passed by. I was very careful not to step on the rose petals because everyone knew something terrible would happen if you did.

Then, running back on the sidewalk again, I turned to see just how close Speedo was, but instead I saw that Speedo had stopped to crouch behind a tree.

He must be tired, I thought, as I headed for a hiding place behind a large hedge. From behind the hedge, I could see that Speedo was staring at something down the street next to me.

I saw what drew Speedo's attention. It was Smiley Loco and the Eastside gang in their car, a '51 Chevy, lowered to four inches off the ground, with a dull black primer paint job and polished chrome bumpers and skirts. They were cat-calling, trying to get a skinny girl into their car with their trash talk. It was Esther, Big Toben's sister, walking like a queen with an off-the-shoulder stare for the *vatos* from Eastside.

I saw Speedo turn and run back, unseen by Eastside.

"Hey, *chula*, come on, honey. You know you wanna ride with me," called Smiley Loco, talking from the left side of his mouth because his lips were frozen from birth in a lop-sided wedge, a fixed curled sneer that showed his yellow, rotting teeth. The car stopped and Smiley Loco, followed by four other boys in trench coats, slowly got out of the car and circled Esther, like a noose around a neck.

I looked down the street and saw Big Toben turning the corner at a slow trot with a tire iron in one hand and a belt with a padlock hooked to the buckle in the other. Then, from nowhere, Tía Cucuy shuffled out and threw rose petals at him. Big Toben tried to jump out of the way, but some petals got smashed under his feet as he ran by. Tía Cucuy leaned over, sweeping with the fringe of her shawl at the petals on the ground like tea leaves at the bottom of a cup.

Big Toben had planned his attack well. I watched him get near Smiley Loco's empty car. He smashed out the tail-lights with the tire iron and banged dents into the trunk with the padlock swinging high over his head. Then he climbed on to the roof of the Chevy, where he swung the padlock into the windows of the car: first the large back window, then the front and both sides.

When Smiley Loco turned to see what was happening to his car, it seemed as if the pain he felt shot to his stomach. He stood looking like an old garage punching bag bent over from too many heavy blows. The rest of his gang watched speechless beside him.

"Get him! Stop him!" yelled Smiley Loco. His boys circled the car with their switch blades and belts ready. But Big Toben had the high ground, and it was tough to get to him without getting hit from above.

"Come on. You want it, come and get it. Come on," sang Big Toben with a wicked grin.

"The trunk, the trunk," Smiley Loco signaled as he grabbed Esther with one hand and pointed with the other. "Get it out of the trunk."

One of the tall boys pulled the car keys out of his pocket and moved toward the trunk of the car while the others tried to keep Big Toben busy. But when he leaned forward to put the key in the trunk, Big Toben took a roundhouse swing at the boy's head, missing by inches. The belted lock cracked into the trunk with a hollow thud and broke loose as the near-victim fell back on his butt to the street.

"You want it, come and get it," shouted Big Toben, even louder now that he had lost his best weapon.

"Open the trunk," Smiley commanded. Now as one of the Eastside boys reached for the trunk, Big Toben could do nothing but watch as it opened. "Okay, okay, get it out," urged Smiley. "Give it to me."

I clenched my fists and walked out from behind the

hedge to help Big Toben. Just when I decided to make my move, Speedo and about twelve others came running down the street toward the car.

"Let's go. Move it!" yelled Smiley Loco when he spotted the Big Arroyo gang coming towards him. As the car doors swung open, Smiley pushed Esther to the ground and jumped into the back seat. The dented Chevy, with an angry Big Toben still on top, started up and pulled away from the curb. Using all his weight, his black curls flopping, Big Toben, jumped up and down on the weak roof of the car until it started to caved in, smashing the heads of those below. When the Chevy gained speed, he reached for the low branch of a Maple tree near the curb and lifted himself from the car as it sped off.

"And don't come back!" Big Toben yelled as he swung from the tree to the ground, where his gang and sister were waiting for him.

I escaped along the hedges, unnoticed, out of sight.

CHAPTER 3

"Up on the Roof"

—The Drifters

"**W**hy does Uncle Joe always have to butt in?" I looked at my mother, knowing she had nothing to do with it.

"Because he's your father's oldest brother." My mother looked calm. "He's only trying to help. Someone has to look out for you—for us."

"But I don't want to live with him," I said as I slumped in the dining room chair across the table from my mother. "I'll split before I'd live with him."

"He didn't say you had to. He was just asking," my mother said. "After all, he has three boys of his own. He thought you might like living with them."

"No, I don't want to go," I continued softly. "I want to stay here with you, my family, where I belong."

"Okay, okay, but I get worried when I hear about you getting into trouble," she said.

"What trouble?" I asked, stubborn as Jello powder stuck to the roof of my mouth.

"Your teacher, Miss Johnson, called about the trouble on the bus," my mother said gently. "She says you'll have to walk the rest of the semester."

"I don't care. I'll walk," I grunted.

"Miss Johnson seems real nice," my mother said. "Do you like her?"

"She's okay."

"We had a long talk about you," she continued. "She likes you very much, I think."

I shrugged my shoulders and stared back at my mother's face.

"At your father's funeral, when I met her, I knew she was a good person." My mother appeared careful, like a school nurse about to give a shot. "She said to let you know that if you ever needed someone to talk to . . ."

"I don't." I ended it, squeezing my eyes shut against the pain.

"And Mrs. Rosas called to tell me that she saw you and Robert killing birds." My mother searched my eyes. "I told her it couldn't be true because you, just like your father, love birds, raise pigeons."

"No, we didn't kill any birds," I said, leaning toward her across the table. "My brown roller pigeon was free-falling, spinning through the air, when it blacked-out and hit the hood of her car."

"What? How does that happen?" my mother asked.

"I don't know, except that Dad used to say the rollers were like children who didn't know any better, risking everything just for kicks. I've got to go outside to feed the pigeons."

Besides, I needed some time to think. On the roof with the pigeons was the best place I knew to do that.

From now on we have to stay away from Big Toben and out of his territory, Big Arroyo, I thought as I sat on the roof of my house in Little Arroyo. I also felt that the rivalry was only a cat and mouse game between the two barrios. Anyway, I, as well as the rest of the boys from Little Arroyo, was expected to fill the ranks of "Big" when we reached high school. Big Arroyo was an old neighborhood, dripping with history and tradition, like an old war movie. Little Arroyo was a new tract of government housing built where cabbage fields used to be. The rivalry was real enough, but sporting, like a fight between brothers of one family. Big Toben, like an older brother, would soon forget about the dead pigeon. But how long would it take? I wondered.

Overlooking my barrio, Little Arroyo, I saw to the south Temple Avenue, a wide street that bordered Arroyo County Park, the buffer between Little and Big Arroyo. A freeway fence lined with trees was the boundary to the north. And on hot summer nights I could see the movie glow from the Tumbleweed Drive-In, lighting the sky to the west. To the east, "The Fields," Mr. Yashida's ten acre vegetable garden always had neat rows planted with cabbage, cauliflower, chard, cantaloupe, and sometimes roses, with a fragrance so strong it stuck to your hair when you walked by, like "Tres Flores" pomade.

I often climbed up to the roof in the evening to bring my pigeons home, and to think—about the past mostly. Lying on my back, hands behind my head, I recalled meeting Robert two years ago. We fought over a seat in the bus, but when neither one would give in, we became friends. Soon we were doing everything together. In the seventh grade, we shared the same girlfriend, picked fights with the same boy. And after one of us would beat him up, the other would, too. In the eighth grade, we co-captained the football, basketball, and baseball teams. We bragged a lot and knew many people didn't like us because we thought we were "it."

The outstretched wings flapping and fluttering overhead pulled me back from my thoughts. I sat up as my cooing pigeons circled around me like a host of angels.

"Okay, your dinner is coming," I soothed. "Let's wait for the others. Go wait in the coop." I clapped my hands, and the pigeons whirled above my head like smoke, then flew down to the coop.

My thoughts went back to the night of my father's death. My forty-four-year-old father died of a heart attack in his sleep. He was a small man with tiny brown eyes and a broad smile of straight teeth. He was a truck driver. After eighteen years of driving, the road atlas was his Bible. Much like the pigeons, his knowledge of roads, streets, freeways, and highways was in his blood. He knew every intersection by its landmarks. A remembered bank building, store, hamburger stand or barber shop was connected in his mind with the names of the streets where they stood.

Again the flapping of wings and soft cooing drew me away from my thoughts as the late ones gathered about me.

"And you, you were my father's favorite," I said, rubbing the breast feathers of a large, full-feathered breeder. "Go on home to the coop. I'll feed all of you in a minute." Once again my loud clap sent them to their backyard perches in the coop behind the house.

Then I remembered how much my father loved the road. He noticed things about the road that nobody else did. He'd mention the whiteness of the concrete on a new freeway before it turned black from use. When someone mentioned the intersection by chance, he told me about the fifty-year history of a brick warehouse on Sixth and Evergreen. A broken freeway guard rail made him think about an auto accident where a child was killed.

It was no surprise to me that my father wanted to be remembered in the same way. After delivering the two twelve-foot gold seals that hang at the entrance of the Los Angeles City Hall, he asked: "After I'm gone, whenever you see those seals, you'll think of me, won't you?"

The cooing from the coop got my attention. Something was scaring the pigeons. Looking at them, I spotted the trouble: A marbled orange and white cat stalked the huddled pigeons in their opened cages. The cat climbed the wall near the coop and crept slowly towards the birds. The birds pecked at the seeds and strutted in tight circles.

The cat stopped, frozen, waiting and choosing.

"Scat!" I yelled as I climbed down from the roof, waving my arms in crazy circles. "Get outta here." The cat ran along the wall in quick chile pepper steps. I stopped and remembered how my dad cared for the pigeons, always talking to them as he filled their seed trays.

"Come on," Dad said, "look what I have for you."

Some pigeons would peck and scramble at his call, scattering seeds left and right. Others would seem bored and pay no attention.

"Com'on," he said. "Share and share alike."

"Why do they always come back?" I asked. "Just to eat?"

"Oh no," Dad replied. "They come back because they want to. They could leave one morning and never come back. You know, we've lost a few that way."

I remembered my father's sadness when a pigeon didn't return.

"I hope it was his choice," Dad said, "and not the decision of a hungry cat, or electric wire, or rolling suicide."

I remembered telling my dad how much I wanted to grow up and take care of animals.

"You could be a veterinarian," Dad said. "You'd have to go to college, though."

I looked out into the darkness and felt how far away that dream seemed now.

I filled the seed trays and locked the doors of the coop. Then I went inside the house and phoned Robert.

"Hey, Robert, you know that little trip I wanted to

take?" I listened for any hint of surprise. "I think I'm ready to take off now. Do you want to go with me?"

"Right now?" Robert replied. "What happened so all of the sudden?"

"My Uncle Joe wants me to live with him." I waited.

"Oh, hell." Robert was surprised. "When do you have to move in with him?"

"Well, it's like hanging over me," I replied. "You know, shape up or ship out."

"Well, you know, we still have a lot of things to do before we leave," said Robert.

"What's up?" I asked.

"Speedo called and wanted to make sure we'll be ready for the football game on Saturday—a case of beer for the winner—and they want us to arrange a dance at the school gym," Robert replied.

"You know just what to say to keep me around don't you?" I kidded him. "A football game, I wouldn't miss it. I guess splitting from here will have to wait for a while. See you tomorrow."

Returning to the rooftop, I focused on Arroyo Park. It seemed to be floating in the distance. Seeing the four block area covered with grass, I thought of Big Toben and our one real passion—football. When I was younger I had idolized Big Toben for being on the high school football team, although he was eventually kicked off the team because of bad grades. The park was neutral ground and the place where we played our weekly games. Besides having the usual basketball court and baseball diamond, our park had the kind of grass football field that all players dreamt about. It was thick, carpet-like grass that was watered by automatic sprinklers three times a week. Every evening, the large Rainbird sprinklers would chat-chat-chat, chit-chit-chit, in wide circles late at night. While everyone slept, the grass grew tall, close and thick.

"I know we can beat Big Arroyo this time," I whispered.

Later, inside at dinner I sat in my father's chair at the table with my family as my mother placed large bowls of rice and beans, and a plate of enchiladas in front of us. My mother was a small woman with dark hair that was splashed with little pools of gray near the temples. She moved from the table to the kitchen, then back again, her apron rippling as she walked. She seemed set on feeding us as if nothing else mattered.

I looked at my three sisters and brother as they reached with lighted eyes for their dinner, mewing:

"This smells good."

"Oh boy, enchiladas."

"Look at the rice steaming."

"Pass me the salt."

"Save me some beans."

"David, aren't you going to have any?"

"We each get two."

"Save some for Mom."

My ten-year-old brother sat across from me in the chair I used to sit in. I noticed Henry's tiny boy body had not gone through the growth spurt that was sure to come. His eyes always seemed to be on me—from the morning combing of hair before school, till late at night when I undressed and went to bed. He watched my every move. Then he secretly practiced them, I knew.

"Here, give me David's plate," Rosie said. At twelve years old her green eyes saw everything. "He's just sitting, looking at us, thinking again. I'll serve him."

"Let me," Barbara begged, now eight and wanting to help, too.

I folded my arms and watched them scramble to put food on my plate.

"Remember," I began, now that everyone was eating. I knew what they wanted—a story. "A couple of years ago, Dad and his brothers, Uncle Joe, Uncle Julio, and Uncle Tomás, were here watching the Rams play football on television. They sat on that couch, drinking beer, looking like the three Musketeers in their gray trucker's uniforms when all of a sudden on a big play—a touchdown pass—they stood up together, shouting, then holding their breath, and when the Ram receiver—I think it was Crazy-Legs Hirsch—dropped the ball, they all sat down hard with their full weight and broke the couch, cracked it in half, right down the middle."

"Ooh," Susie cried. My four-year-old sister held her hands to her mouth with a smile.

"Then when Mom ran from the kitchen to see what had happened, she saw the four of them staring at the screen, watching the next Ram's play, leaning shoulder-to-shoulder against each other like four clay pots on a broken shelf, not even noticing what happened."

I looked at my smiling mother standing at the kitchen doorway, watching us laugh. Then I heard the front door open and someone enter. From where I sat I could only see brown leather work boots and gray trucker's pants, like my father used to wear. Now everyone turned to look in that direction.

"Daddy, Daddy," Susie called, saying what everyone was thinking and feeling—it was dinner time and, as usual, Daddy was home from work. She slid down from her chair and ran to greet her father. When she wrapped her arms around his leg, Uncle Joe looked at all of us, scared and dumb.

I rose from my chair, went to Susie, and held her in my arms as she began to cry.

"I just wanted to see if everything's okay," Uncle Joe stuttered. "Do you need anything?"

"Thanks, but everything is fine," I said. "We don't need anything from you."

CHAPTER 4

"Sh-boom"

—The Chords

I sat at a desk at the front of the room, watched and listened, thinking how Mr. West reminded me of Humphrey Bogart.

"Traditionally, the new members are required to provide a small wooden board, a writing tablet, on which they must obtain all the current members' signatures," said Mr. West, the advisor of the Wilson Junior High School "Lettermen's Club." He wore a blue tweed sports coat that fit tight at his shoulders and chest like knight's armor. As he spoke to the club's twenty-four members, he palmed wild short strands of curly black hair behind his left ear.

I remembered Mr. West had once told me that he had been a fighter plane gunner in World War II before becoming a teacher. In college he chose math because it was a subject that was clear-cut, easy to understand. "You see, after working on a problem and arriving at an answer, you're either right or wrong. There's no maybes, or half rights, or half wrongs. It's either right or wrong! That's what I like about mathematics," Mr. West had said. As head coach of all inter-school sports for boys, Mr. West was famous. He was a strict and demanding leader whose teams won championships and everyone expected it, especially in football. I thought Mr. West liked me and my friends, but sometimes, I thought he didn't.

"Now, you can make a new member work for your signature a letter at a time, if you want." Mr. West's voice drew my attention. "You can make the recruit earn a letter of your name by making him do special deeds for you. But keep it within reason. Like running into the girl's restroom shouting, 'Fire! Fire!' but don't send him into the principal's office to steal his marble desk pen set or into Miss Johnson's room to take her board pointer. Besides, these things have been done before and they'll be ready for you."

A howl of laughter filled the room, but as soon as things died down, I noticed Mr. West's face turn to stone. "That's enough about recruitment," he said. "I know a tackle football game between Little Arroyo and Big Arroyo is planned for a week from this Saturday. I just want to say this: Use common sense. In a sandlot game, without protective equipment, someone's bound to get hurt. And I don't want it to be one of you boys. Get my point? If I thought I could make it stick, I'd forbid you to play with the Big Arroyo gang at all." West cocked his bushy eyebrows and stared at Robert and me.

For us the message was clear. As president and vice-president of the club, Robert and I would be held responsible if Mr. West's advice wasn't obeyed by all our members.

After the meeting, Mr. West took both of us aside. "I'm getting you both out of class to line the field for tomorrow's championship football game. After all, you owe me a favor. One person could do it, but I wouldn't want to separate the Gold Dust Twins," said Mr. West. "The limer and two sacks of lime are in the custodian's shed near the field. Do a neat job."

"Why do we owe you a favor?" I didn't miss my cue.

"Because I got the gym for Friday's dance approved by the principal."

I thought that the lime spreader was a neat machine. It looked like an upside down metal pyramid with one metal wheel at the bottom. The two handles at the top let me push it like a cart. After the pyramid was filled with lime, a release lever near the handle let the lime run through a small trap door at the bottom. By pushing the limer slowly along with the door open, I made a narrow white line appear on the ground below the limer.

"Hey, Robert, come take this limer. You know how it works, right? You've got to follow the old lines of the field."

Robert gave the limer a try.

"Okay, take it easy. I'm doing it." Robert pushed the limer faster, forcing me to jump aside as I tried to guide the limer in front.

"Don't fool around, Robert. You almost ran over my toes."

"Well, get out of my way!" said Robert, pulling the trap door lever closed. He stopped moving. "Look, do you want to do it? Or are you going to let me do it?"

"No. I can see better than you can, but that's okay. You go on making your crooked lines."

"You can see better than I can? Is that so!" said Robert. "Well, tell me then, eagle eye, who's the best looking between Esther and Rhonda?"

"Esther."

"Ha, ha. Don't make me laugh," said Robert leaning on the handle of the limer. "She's flat-chested and chicken-legged. But Rhonda's got a body. She's stacked and you know it."

"My, you do need new glasses, my boy," I said, talking like our teacher, Miss Johnson, in a high voice.

"Oh yeah? Start running, David," said Robert as he pushed the limer into me. "I'll put a nice straight white line down the middle of your back!"

I dashed off in a zigzag pattern, trying to get away. Right behind me, Robert rattled the limer, matching me move for move. When I began to run in large circles, Robert did his best to cut me off. One time Robert hit my heel with the front wheel, causing me to tumble to the ground. I bounced back on my feet by doing a somersault and continued running without losing my stride. Robert chased close behind. Spotting a large chuck hole at mid-field, I carefully led Robert there. At the last minute, with a quick turn of my heel, I cut like a halfback to the right, missing the hole. Robert was not as lucky. He and the limer hit the hole at top speed, causing the limer to tip over on its side and Robert to go head over heels in midair. He landed on his back, unhurt.

"I didn't see it. I didn't see it," shouted Robert between fits of laughter.

"I know. You're blind. I told you so!" I stood looking down at Robert. We shook with laughter. Then I looked at the field around us. Robert stood up and looked where I looked. I was staring at a green football field that was covered with white lines in crazy patterns of curves and zig-zags. The limer had been open during the entire chase.

"Oh, no!"

"Oh, yes!"

Robert and I fell to the ground with laughter. As we lay on our backs, arms outspread, it felt like we were floating on a green sea of grass while all around us the white lines formed eddies and swirls that spun our bodies around and around. We were in the center of something big, bigger than both of us, spinning with laughter.

Looking into the pale sky, I saw the roller pigeons soaring, silently waiting for their turn, and I felt like I was one of them.

"When are you two going to get serious about things, about life? You can't just wander aimlessly looking for fun," Mr. West said, as he placed his forearms on his desk, leaning forward toward Robert and me as we sat across from him. "What you did to that field was crazy. Sometimes you act as though you don't have any sense, but I know better. You've got smarts, use them."

I caught Mr. West's eye.

"Do you understand?" Mr. West asked.

"Yes," I replied. Robert remained silent next to me.

"Well, I don't know how I'll get you out of this mess—the principal is pretty upset—but I'll try . . ."

"Thanks, Mr. West," I said.

"Okay, boys. You're excused," sighed Mr. West.

We jumped up from our chairs like two freed birds while Mr. West shook his head and smiled.

At home, I fed the pigeons, then sat on the ground in front of the coop. I thought about what my father had said, "You can learn a lot from the pigeons."

I decided I wanted to talk to someone, anyone. Decisions aren't easy to make by yourself, I thought.

"Okay, I'll talk to all of you," I said to the pigeons. "I know I can get hurt playing football with the gang, but I don't care. I love playing. I like the feeling of running across an open field. The freedom. You should understand that. You have the sky all to yourselves." I waited for them to do something, give me a signal. "And I like being with my friends. Having fun with them, laughing, joking, playing hard. You ought to understand that, too—the way you fly all together in a covey, over trees and rooftops. And the fun you have together playing your rolling game in the air."

Again, silence was everywhere, except for the soft cooing as I waited for their answer. "I know Mr. West is right. I could get hurt playing football, just as you could get hurt rolling through the air with your wings closed. But you still do it. Why? For me, playing football is fun and nothing else matters when I'm playing, except running, tackling, and trying to score a touchdown."

Frustrated by their silence, I stood up and slowly waved the back of my hand at the birds as I turned and headed for the house. Now my mind switched to the problem of getting a case of beer if my gang lost the football game to Big Arroyo. El Wino, the old man who always hung out at the Thunderbird Bar next to Mickey's Liquor store, would buy it for me, but where was I going to get the money?

"Golf balls, golf balls," I whispered as I went to the phone to call Robert.

CHAPTER 5

"La Bamba"

—Ritchie Valens

Before dawn a knock at the window let me know that Robert was there. I opened the front door quietly. In my hands I held two pieces of *pan dulce*.

"Here's breakfast," I said handing a piece of *pan dulce* to Robert. "Where's your jacket?"

"Who needs one? Feel how nice and warm it is," he said

"You're right. It is warm, but at 4:30 in the morning?"

"It's the wind."

I felt the Santa Ana winds brush through the night like a warm summer breeze. Through the shaking leaves I saw the clear black sky dotted with stars, like thousands of cat eyes blinking in the dark. I remembered the Santa Ana winds were called the devil winds because of their strange warmth and strength.

After climbing the chain link fence that surrounded the Los Angeles Golf Course, Robert and I walked slowly over the dry tall grass to the clump of castor bean trees that ran along the thirteenth fairway. We decided to lie down and rest in the tall grass, but the warm wind and moonlight were too exciting. It was impossible to sleep.

Without speaking, I rose, stretched, and began walking; Robert followed. We headed across the fairway down a small hill toward the lake. The damp moss odor signaled we were close.

"I can't see it, but it must be here," Robert said.

"I can't see a thing."

I stepped slowly, fearing that at any moment I would step in the lake that was hidden in the darkness. With one cautious step, my toe kicked a pebble that plopped into the lake. With that, the drumming of a hundred wings beat in our ears. The deafening explosion sent us sprinting blindly for cover into the night.

Hearing the terrified birds squawking above, we stopped.

"Ducks!" I said.

"You scared the ducks that were sleeping on the pond."

"Yeah, and they scared us!" I said, laughing and trying to catch my breath.

"Let's get back to the castor beans where it's safe."

"As soon as I catch my breath," I replied.

Later, our hands were deep in the grass beneath the castor bean trees searching for golf balls. Because the grass was deep, I knew the stray balls were quickly given up for lost by a golfer not willing to get down on his hands and knees to search. We each took an area at opposite sides of the clump, moving slowly on all fours to the middle. Within twenty minutes, I had found five balls and Robert had found eight. Robert found one that looked really good, maybe hit only once before it was lost. The black nick did not look like it cut the shiny skin. A good scrubbing would be the only way to know for sure, I thought.

I saw that no one was on the course yet. I knew we were safe now, but we had to work quickly. We had only a half-hour before the golf pro would arrive. Searching for the balls was not illegal, but trespassing on private property was. We moved to the fence that bordered the wash, the San Gabriel Channel. We found twelve more balls in the weeds.

"Let's get these scrubbed, then look them over and see what we have."

"Okay."

At the eighth hole, we put the balls into the scrubber. Then we dried and buffed the balls with our T-shirts.

"Dave, look at this one. It's a Titleist Red Dot!"

"A what?"

"A Titleist Red Dot without a mark on it. It's been hit only once. It will bring me as much money as all nine of your balls together."

"Sure. You're dreaming, Robert," I said. "I just hope we earn enough to pay for the case of beer if we lose the football game."

"You'll see. Let's just wait for our first customer. It's about seven o'clock now. The pro must be here. You keep your eyes open for him."

We sat on a short wooden bench, keeping an eye on the clubhouse.

"Hey, Robert, look over there." I pointed to a groundskeeper riding high on a yellow tractor about fifty yards away.

"Don't worry about him. He won't say anything." Robert waved to the dark Mexican man. From behind the wheel of the tractor, he waved back.

We had been making deals for about an hour when a golfer came near. We approached him with our goods in hand.

"Would you like to buy some good practice balls cheap?" asked Robert, holding out the shiny balls in his hands.

"Well," the bald golfer picked up a couple of the balls. "I don't need practice balls. Do you have anything better?"

"Yeah." Robert pulled the Titleist Red Dot from his pocket. He flashed it slowly beneath the golfer's eyes.

"Hmmm."

"It's like new. Probably only been hit once. Like it?"

"How much?"

"A dollar seventy-five." Robert looked the man right in the eye.

"Does Gus the pro know you're here?" the golfer asked as he squeezed the ball in his hand.

"The price is five dollars." Robert took the ball back. "The same price that Gus the pro would charge you if he had it to sell."

"Well, I didn't mean any . . ." The golfer's words were drowned out by a distant shout.

"¡Miren, miren!" shouted the Mexican man as he stood on top of his tractor and pointed.

I looked in the direction he was pointing. A police squad car roared down the dirt pathway towards us, beating a cyclone of dust into the air.

"No deal!" Robert clutched his Red Dot and dashed across the fairway toward the fence that bordered the wash. I was close behind. As we neared the green, we came close to being run over by a golf cart driven by an old man.

"Here you go!" said Robert as he pressed the Titleist Red Dot into the surprised man's hand. "Have a nice day!"

Safe beyond the concrete walls of the wash, we sat under a small grove of orange trees. We breathed in deep and talked about our narrow escape.

"It was a good thing that gardener was on the lookout," I said, holding a large orange about the size of a grapefruit in my hand.

"Yeah," said Robert. "The old pro almost caught us this time."

"He called the police?"

"Sure he did. He can't stand to see somebody else make money on practice balls," said Robert as he bit into an orange and tried to peel it with his teeth. "Yuck! This orange is sour!"

"Mine, too!"

We ate them anyway.

"My lips feel strange," Robert said. "Like I was kissing a window pane."

"Your lips look strange too. I guess the sourness made them pucker."

"Yours look puckered, too."

"Let's get some water," I said as I got up and ran out from under the shade of the trees.

The grove ended by a large grassy field that was now flooded with water. The irrigation water ran across the ground, sending waves across several acres. We ran through the grass toward the growing pool of water. Dunking our heads in the bubbling water softened our puckered lips a little bit, and refreshed us enough to start the walk home. We walked across the flooded field holding our shoes and socks.

"Go out for a pass!" I called to Robert who was leading the way. As Robert sprinted to the left, I threw a perfect shoulder-high pass with an orange I had saved. Robert caught it with his free hand.

"Hit me!" I ran across the water kicking up sprays and splashing. It was a low pass. I dived for it, dropping my shoes and socks and doing a belly-flop on top of the water. But I held onto the orange.

"I caught it!" I yelled as I sat up in the water, holding the "ball" high in my right hand. When I saw Robert bent over with laughter, I realized that my shoes and socks were floating a couple of yards away. "Oh, no. My shoes are all wet!"

"You're all wet!" Robert said between bursts of laughter.

I stood up, then charged toward Robert, tackling him at the waist and driving him across the flooded ground. Robert stopped laughing. He pulled at my T-shirt, trying to get himself free. I rolled over, taking Robert with me. Robert got back on his feet just in time for me to trip him again. We both jumped up, but when Robert grabbed at my T-shirt to keep his balance, the shirt tore. I got back at him by tearing his T-shirt. We both ripped and pulled until both shirts were in shreds. Naked to our waists, sitting in six inches of water, we held our heads back, laughing, until our sides ached.

CHAPTER 6

"The Great Pretender"

—The Platters

When we got back to Robert's house, he was surprised to see his father at home. This time Robert's father had been gone for two months.

"Where have you been, Robert?" asked his father, Carlos. He was a dark, big-shouldered man with a large straight nose and dark eyes.

"Out with David," replied Robert as we walked to his room at the end of the hallway.

"Since four o'clock in the morning?" his father continued. He sat at the dining room table. A coffee cup steamed beneath his hairy nostrils. "Come here and answer me!"

I remembered that when Robert was younger he always believed his mother's explanation about his father's long periods away from home.

"Your father must follow the harvests. Many times he has to go upstate to pick crops."

Back then, his father's homecoming was a time of fun and laughter. His arms would be full of gifts for everyone, he would walk through the door like a giant returning from faraway places to share strange presents with his family. For days Robert would brag about his father's return throughout the neighborhood. He was proud then, I remembered.

But as Robert grew older, he realized that his mother was not telling the whole truth. His father was gone a lot of the time because he liked to drink. He came home only when he was "short on money and long on guilt," some neighbors would say. It looked to me like Robert wasn't happy that his father was back.

Robert kept walking and I followed. When we reached his room, we dropped onto Robert's bed and fell asleep until dinner time. After we ate, we returned to Robert's room and listened to some of his records, Fats Domino and Ritchie Valens. I called my Mom to let her know I was going to stay the night.

Hours later, I felt the bed move and woke up to the sound of a voice.

"Wake up, Robert," Carlos said. "We're going fishing off the rocks below the cliffs at Portuguese Bend."

Raised up on an elbow, I saw Robert's father step out of the room as Robert sat upright on the edge of his bed.

"It's three o'clock in the morning." Robert stared at the clock in disbelief.

"It's still dark outside."

"Do you want to go fishing with us, David?" Robert asked. "My father always takes us fishing before he leaves again."

"Fishing?"

"Yeah, we'll be back by noon, I think."

"Yeah, I want to go." I added, " My mom knows I'm with you. It should be all right."

"Carlos, here's your coffee," said Alicia to her husband as we drove along the dark highway. I sat with Robert in the back seat, trying to sleep, but listening all the time.

"Did you get any more calls?" Carlos asked.

"Yes, but only two."

"Those bastards. Why can't they stay off my back? I've got enough problems."

"It's okay, Carlos. I talked to them. I explained."

"Explained what? Hell, they know everything. Bunch of smart guys. Let them take the furniture. It's all crap anyway."

"Carlos, I think the car ahead of us is going to turn."

"I see it, Alicia. I see it. Move that piece of junk! Get the hell-outta-the-way!"

"He's turning, Carlos. He's turning."

"I know, Alicia. I know."

Stomping on the gas pedal, Carlos, moving to the left, breezed past the turning car and sped down the deserted highway. No one spoke for an hour or more.

I watched as Carlos rolled down the car window to spit out the phlegm that he had noisily gathered in his throat.

"Could you roll the window up again, please Carlos? It's cold. The boys are sleeping in the back seat," Alicia asked.

Carlos rolled up the window without a word.

But the cold night air had already found its way to the back seat, and I sat up straight and yawned. Robert leaned forward and rested his elbows on the back cushion of the front seat.

"Are we almost there, Dad?"

"Yeah, almost. Did you bring your work boots, like I told you? We're going to be out on the rocks."

Robert remained silent.

"Well, did you, Robert?"

"I . . . I . . . I forgot . . ."

"Damn! Robert, don't you ever listen? Why can't you do as I tell you . . . just once? Damn it!"

"Carlos, have some more coffee," said Alicia.

Robert slumped down in the corner of the back seat.

"He didn't want to tell you, Carlos," whispered Alicia. "His boots are worn out, the soles falling apart. He couldn't wear them, but he didn't want to bother you about that."

"What kind of shoes did you bring?" Carlos asked without turning his eyes from the road.

"Tennis shoes. I thought . . ."

"Yeah, okay. The rubber soles will grip well to wet rocks."

Robert leaned to one side and went to sleep. I folded my arms across my chest and soon fell asleep, too.

I woke up when I felt the car swerve. Looking out the window, I saw that we were nearing a moonlit field of mustard weeds. Carlos turned onto the dirt shoulder on the left. The sound of crickets grew louder as the rumble of the dying engine faded when Carlos took the key out of the ignition.

"Wake the boys, Alicia. Let's get started. It's five o'clock. The tide is about right."

"We're up. We're up," Robert and I called out together.

Stepping from the car, Carlos turned up the collar of his jacket to the cold salt wind. He then walked to the back of the car and opened the trunk.

With all of our help, Carlos took three fishing poles from the trunk, a tackle box, a large two-gallon thermos jug, a claw hammer and a bucket. Loaded down with gear, Carlos walked to an opening in a barbed wire fence. We followed. He stepped on a fallen, wooden "No Trespassing" sign as he passed through the fence into a narrow gully that snaked through the field. We were close behind him, but Alicia walked a little farther back. No one talked, but I felt like we were on some kind of treasure hunt and only we knew where to find the treasure.

Reaching the end of the field, we stopped at the edge of a hundred-foot cliff. I saw below, the sea crashing on the shore, leaving big fans of surf that looked like foam from exploding pop bottles on the sand.

Carlos went first as we slowly walked down a dusty steep, narrow trail. We stepped carefully on the path that zig-zagged back and forth. Halfway down to the bottom, Alicia lost her footing in the soft dirt. She dropped the brown bag of supplies as she fell, sliding on her back, down past Robert and me. Carlos, reaching for her helpless body, caught her by the hair, and stopped her fall to the rocky beach below. We all helped her up.

"I'm sorry, Carlos."

Without saying a word, he took her hand and led her the rest of the way to the beach. Robert and I followed.

On the beach, we picked up the fallen supplies and walked to the pebbled edge of a cove surrounded by two cliffs that stuck out like black shards of glass slicing out into the sea.

"We've got plenty of time. The tide is low enough now. We should be able to get all the mussels we need," Carlos said. "Come this way."

Carlos took the trail on the left that led to the cliff. The wet wall of the cliff was slippery and dangerous. Small, sharp, pointed rocks were stuck between large wet, flat ones, making the way slow. Robert and I were the first to reach the finger of rocky land that stretched from the bottom of the cliff into the sea.

When Alicia caught up, Carlos told her to wait there while we got the mussel from the rocks that we would use for bait.

"Alicia, David will be back with a full bucket of mussel. You shell them. Use this big hunting knife," Carlos said.

Carrying his hammer and bucket, Carlos walked the narrow strip of sandy ground, like a tightrope, out into the water. Robert and I followed. I turned and looked back at the mass of boulders that were huddled on all sides like scared giants suffering loud slaps from the rising tide.

"Listen, Robert, I'm going the rest of the way out there by myself. Give me the hammer. David, keep the bucket and wait here. I'll be down there on those rocks with my back to the tide. Robert keep your eyes on those waves. Warn me when a big one is going to hit. Remember the tide'll be rising all the time. I'm depending on you. In another hour those rocks will be under eight feet of water."

"I'll be watching Dad," said Robert as he watched Carlos walk away.

Standing with a bucket in my hand, I watched as Carlos leaped from rock to rock over the tide pools. Spotting a gang of large mussel growing on rocks in shallow water, Carlos, with his back to the sea, planted his large legs and feet as firmly as possible on the wet boulders. He raised the claw hammer high above his head, and came down hard, driving the steel spikes into the black shells. The force of the blow caused bits of broken shell to burst into the air, making a pink juice ooze out like guts from a belly wound. He yanked, pulled, and pried until they came loose. Carlos tossed the pack of mussel into the waiting bucket I held about fifteen feet away. He carefully aimed every swing of his strong arm, always missing the younger mussel. Their small size made them useless as bait, but he didn't want to kill them.

"Look out, Dad! Here comes one!"

Quickly, Carlos ran to the safety of the higher ground as the tall waves fell down on the rocks.

Looking from the crashing wave to Robert, Carlos nodded his head. He then went back to his place on the rocks below.

He worked steadily and was only stopped by Robert's shouts. When the bucket was filled to spilling fullness, he asked me to take it to Alicia. When I reached her, I dumped the mussels at her feet, then returned to Carlos and Robert.

From a distance I looked back and watched as Alicia, kneeling, broke one mussel free from the others. Using a sharp knife, Alicia pried the shell open at the seams. She then scraped the pink-red jelly creature out and cut its black nervy knot from the shell into a plastic bag. As she worked, the morning sky lighted a yellow dust around her form. From high cliff ledges above her, seagulls with wings outspread leaped into the air. Flying low, they squealed and cawed while eyeing the gutted mussel shells scattered about Alicia's feet.

Later, I saw Robert bending over to get a bunch of mussel that had been thrown short of my bucket. He grabbed the shells, and smiling, raised them above his head to show me. But, when he looked towards his father, his body froze with fear when he saw a big wave coming like a speeding train a short distance behind his father.

"Look out, Dad!"

Without turning, Carlos ran up the slippery rocks as a blast of tide hit his back, knocking him spread-eagle against a colony of mussel. The shells cut into his skin like broken glass as the tide poured over him. With his right hand he stubbornly gripped the wooden handle of the hammer that had been driven into the mussel with the force of his fall. The receding tide sucked at him. He clung like a leech to the army of piercing shells with his whole body. Losing the battle, he seemed to gather all his remaining strength in his surfaced right arm and struck a fresh blow with the hammer into the mass of mussel. He was clinging to the hammer with both hands above his head as the tide ebbed, sinking its liquid weight down his shoulders, back, legs, ankles, and feet.

"Dad! Dad!"

Robert and I raced to his Dad, helping him to his feet and up to the safety of higher ground. His wet clothes sticking to his chest, thighs, and back, Carlos shivered in the breeze. At his right side, the hammer stuck out from his tightened fist as if it were a part of him.

"Pick up the bucket, David," said Carlos as he went back to his spot on the rocks. The bucket continued to be filled and emptied a lot of times before Carlos went to Alicia and said:

"That's enough. We have enough bait to last all day."

"Yes, Carlos."

As the morning sun grew hotter, we took off our jackets and sweaters, tying them by the sleeves around our waists. Picking up our gear, the four of us returned along the rocky shore, rounded the cove and headed toward the cliff on the other side.

"Be careful, Robert," shouted Alicia. When Robert and I had safely reached her, we set our gear down at the foot of the rocks. Carlos, on one knee, opened his tackle box and began fixing his deep-sea fishing pole. He put two number six hooks on an eight-inch leader. Old spark plugs were used for weights. He put the mussel on the end of the barbed hooks by jabbing the knot of black cord. He then helped Alicia with her pole; Robert and I fixed our own.

When Carlos climbed to the top of the wall of rocks, we followed. The loud waves broke against the boulders, sending a salt spray that slapped my face. I watched as Carlos set his feet firmly apart and heaved the weighted line over his right shoulder into the air and out to sea. We found our spots a few feet away and made good casts, too. Looking out across the bright, reflected light of the sea, we waited quietly under the hot sun.

After five-and-a-half hours, we had caught eight fish, five by Carlos and one each for the rest of us. Carlos, shirtless, sat silently looking at his stiff line dance on the water's surface. Robert and I rested with our poles ready. Robert's mother went down to the picnic bag to get some sandwiches for us.

When she came back, I saw someone following behind her. He was carrying a small freshwater reel and pole, and a new blue plastic tackle box. A funny straw hat was stuck on his head. It had a slot in the band where he kept a pack of cigarettes and matches. On the front of his hat a red button

said: "Beer Bust" and across his new yellow shirt was sten-
ciled: Cal State L.A. His faded corduroy pants were cut off
about a half-foot above his blue tennis shoes, showing a pair
of white sweat socks. Walking quickly, he came and sat next
to us. Robert's Dad just gave him a lazy glance.

The guy found a spot near Carlos and set his gear down.
I watched as he knelt beside his tackle box. Opening it, he
pulled out a bag of Kraft mini-marshmallows and stuck several of them on to a pair of treble hooks at the end of his line.

"College fool," grumbled Carlos, seeing the way he
baited his hook.

The guy didn't even cast his baited line out to sea, but
just dropped it down between the rocks and watched the
tiny marshmallows sink into the saltwater below. In a few
minutes he reeled in a huge opal-eye. I couldn't believe it.

"Beginner's luck," whispered Carlos.

But the guy was able to catch twelve large fish in less
than an hour and a half, while we caught only one.

I noticed that Carlos didn't pay much attention at first.
But, as the strange fisherman began reeling in large catch-
es, Carlos grew uneasy. As the sun grew hotter, we waited,
catching nothing, not even a nibble.

"Can we change our bait from mussel to marshmallows,
Dad?" asked Robert.

Carlos answered in cold silence, like a bite into a *ras-
pada* of shaved ice.

Finally, the guy packed up his stuff and left, carrying
his string of fish by his side. We stayed for two and a half

hours more, changing our fishing spot from rock to rock, trying to find the fishing hole.

"The fish have stopped biting, Carlos. Do you think we can go home now?" asked Alicia. Her skin was raw and red from the many hours out in the sun and salt.

After picking up the gear, we followed Carlos down from the rocks, stepping across the tide pools, and headed along the cliff to the cove's beach. From there we walked up the footpath to the field. We walked across the field without talking. As we came near our parked car, I saw the guy's tossed string of fish rotting in the sun near a wooden fence post. Carlos walked by the wasted fish without saying a word.

At home everyone, now rested and showered, sat at the dinner table. Steam rose above our plates of Spanish rice and fish fillets as we ate. Robert's mother didn't look beyond her fork and spoon and kept her head bowed. Robert and I ate the fish like it was our last meal on earth. Rising from the table after dinner, I heard Carlos ask Robert to get his coat, suitcase, and grip.

"I should be there by Sunday night. I'll send you some money as soon as I can. And don't worry. You'll be all right. Right, Alicia?"

"Yes, Carlos. Don't worry. We'll be okay. You take care of yourself. We'll be all right."

"Yeah . . . yeah. I guess so." Carlos spoke softly. "Bye, Alicia."

"Bye, Carlos."

Carlos took his coat and suitcase from Robert as he approached. I watched as Robert, carrying the grip, followed his father across the living room and out the front door. Alicia and I looked on from the front doorstep as Carlos put his coat and suitcase in the back seat of the car.

Taking the grip from Robert, Carlos set it on the ground at his feet. Putting his hands to Robert's shoulders, he hugged him hard enough to squeeze him dry. Robert's eyes filled with tears. I could see that his breathing became rough, making him suck in air like a beached fish.

"Take me with you, Dad," begged Robert.

"No, no, stay . . . make it . . . make it here . . . be here . . . live here . . . help . . ."

Carlos got into his car and sped away, leaving Robert with his head in his hands, surrounded by the sick sound of screeching tires and the rotten smell of burnt rubber.

I walked to Robert's side and put my arm around his shoulder. His mother waited for him at the doorstep and then walked him inside as I turned and went home.

Later in my room, I emptied my pockets on my bed. I had eighty-five cents in change and a one dollar bill.

"Not enough for a case of beer," I sighed. Then I walked to the kitchen where my mother was making tortillas.

"Do you think you could give me a couple of dollars, Mom?" I asked as I sat on a stool near the stove.

"Oh, I didn't hear you walk in," my mother replied. "*Me asustaste.* Have you been at Robert's all this time?" She wrung her hands on her apron and looked down. "I don't have any money, David. I was just now thinking about borrowing some money to pay bills and other things."

"Borrow money?" I asked. "Borrow from who?"

"Your Uncle Joe."

"No, please don't do that," I pleaded. "I'll get a job. A full-time job. I'll quit school."

"Oh, no," my mother replied. "You can't quit school. We'll borrow the money. It'll be all right."

"Please, don't," I begged, standing now with my shoulders hunched. "I'll sell the pigeons. I can get a lot of money for them." I didn't wait for her answer. I ran out the door to the backyard where the pigeon coop stood. I counted my birds: eighteen kips, twelve breeders, and ten rollers.

"Two hundred dollars," I said. "Mr. García on the next block has always wanted them. He'll buy them. I'm sure he will."

After I sold my pigeons, I gave the money to my mother and felt that I had made the right decision for my family.

At dinner I sat quietly. Rosie, Henry and Barbara knew something was wrong. They kept their heads down, looking into their plates, waiting for a sign. In the kitchen, my mother peeked over her shoulder, hoping that I would be all right.

"Remember when Rosie won that bike on the television show, 'Hail the Champ'?" I began.

"Yeah, tell us that one." Everyone shouted together, except Rosie who grew shy and smiled from across the table.

"Okay, okay, but you know that story already," I said. "Let me tell you something about the part you haven't heard."

I sat back in my chair and began to tell the story: Weeks before the bike was delivered to the house in the projects, Rosie, Mom, Dad, and I went to Catalina as guests of the Powerhouse Candy Company. It was another one of the prizes Rosie had won on the show.

After walking and sightseeing for hours, we bought some fresh steamed crab legs and sat on the large rocks near the waves. We were tired, but happy.

"I've always wanted to come here," Dad said, looking around at the harbor.

Rosie sat next to him, feeling so proud. She could tell Dad was happy.

"I remember all the deliveries headed for Catalina that I'd unload at the docks early afternoons when, on a clear day, you could see it. Oh, the island sitting out there like a castle or something. Boy, I wanted to go there." Dad parted his lips into a bright smile.

"It is like a dream," Mom said. "Almost like we've been here before. *Qué milagro.*"

"Remember the time I delivered all that Harts Mountain birdseed to the docks headed for Catalina?" Dad asked in Mom's direction. I thought I saw Mom dip her head in a shy way.

"What happened?" Rosie asked, sensing that Dad was ready to tell a story.

"Well, this happened before you were born and David was only two, just a baby. At the Harts Mountain warehouse there were a lot of birds for sale, so I brought one home for your Mom. It was a small yellow canary. And a guy there gave me a record of singing canaries that he said would help get my canary to sing."

"Did it sing?" Rosie asked. Mom and Dad only laughed and shared a look. "Well, I don't know," Dad continued. "You see, about a week later, the bird was left out on the porch in its cage, and the neighbor's cat ate it. Quick as a heartbeat, it was gone."

"Ooh," Rosie gasped, looking to Mom to see if it was true.

"And your mother didn't want me to find out, so she played the canary records all the time, especially when I got home from work." Dad laughed. "It was a long time before I figured out what happened."

"I cried when he found out the canary was gone, and I told him everything." Mom put her hand on Dad's. "He said, 'It's all right, I'll buy you another one someday.'"

"Did he?" Rosie asked.

"I don't know. All I remember is that he said he would. And that was enough."

Then we all laughed so hard our sides hurt.

CHAPTER 7

"The Stroll"

—The Diamonds

Martha, Yolie, the twins, Rachel, Esther, Renee, Anita, Rhonda, Lucy, and just about all the other girls from Big and Little Arroyo were gathered around the table, making posters for Friday night's dance. I watched Mr. West, who looked proud, overlooking what he said was the first real attempt to bring the two gangs together and create peace in the neighborhood.

I stood close by the girls, pointing and making suggestions for colors and wording.

"Donation, one dollar," I said. "We aren't going to really charge admission."

"Yeah, but it's one dollar per couple and two dollars stag," added Speedo, squatting on the ground next to Big Toben, who was smiling at the girls.

The girls worked quietly, dipping small squares of sponge into paint colors, and dabbing them neatly on white poster board to make letters and designs.

Rachel, a short, pale-skinned girl of sixteen, was especially artistic in creating designs on the edges of the poster board. She used her long black hair to brush the paint on the board creating a long wave of greens and blues.

"See what can be accomplished when we all work together?" asked Mr. West, smiling. "If everything works out well with no problems at the dance, we can do more of this kind of thing—dances, car washes, and other events."

We all nodded our heads and smiled.

That night Robert, Big Toben, Speedo, the girls, and I got to the gym early to decorate and set up microphones, record players, and speakers. I looked around the Wilson Jr. High gym that was used as the student cafeteria during the school day. It was a brown and green large rectangular room with transom windows near the ceiling. Two large double doors stood to the right and left of the curtained stage, and a third double door at the rear opened to a garden.

"Are your guys ready for the game Saturday?" Big Toben asked, smiling.

"Yeah, I think so," I replied, reaching for Big Toben's extended hand.

"Say, come over to my house tomorrow," Big Toben said. "We'll go over the game plan together."

"Okay, I'll be there," I replied, trying to shake Big Toben's hand hard.

After the purple and white streamers and multi-colored balloons were hung from the ceiling lights, Mr. West tested the microphone and turntable to check that everything was ready.

"Let me have your attention," Mr. West spoke into the microphone from the stage. "It looks terrific everyone. You did a great job. We have only about fifteen minutes before the dance begins. Miss Johnson, will you please lock all the doors except the one that exits to the parking lot?"

Miss Johnson locked all of the doors securely, then signaled to Mr. West that she was done.

"Okay, remember," Mr. West spoke firmly, "no one can enter or leave this gym except through that door." He pointed to the unlocked door to the left of the stage. "The fire chief won't be happy, but I think it's the safest thing to do, considering the trouble we have had in the past with unwanted gate-crashers."

By now everyone had stopped and turned toward the stage. You need rules for everything, even to have fun, I thought.

"Another thing—when someone buys a ticket, he's here for the night—till the dance is over at midnight. If someone must leave early, he can't return. This will avoid a lot of problems."

The boys all looked at each other, shrugged their shoulders and shook their heads. Mr. West was very cautious—but he let us have the dance, so we went along. As I walked to the door, Speedo started the records spinning.

"La Bamba" was blaring from the gym speakers as

Esther and I stood at the door to collect money for tickets. Even though we were just friends, I was glad to see that my blue plaid Pendleton matched Esther's outfit. She wore a powder blue sweater with an open neck and a tight-fitting black skirt with a short slit at the back. At first, only a few couples arrived. Then, slowly, a line formed as the crowd that wanted to enter the dance grew larger.

"I think we might make some money tonight," I said to Esther, who was moving her feet to the music as she handed the tickets out.

Later, I sat with Esther on stage watching eighty couples dance the Stroll, the Grind and the BeBop beneath the colorful streamers and balloons. Watching the slow movement of the dancers who were pressed together like pairs of wings, I thought of my pigeons—how they huddled together for company, for safety. Were people like that, too? I noticed how the music seemed to calm everyone and send us to another place, another time—warm, hidden, protected. Now as the melodies soothed and the dancers' arms were laced together, holding each other, the troubles of the world seemed far, far away. The rhythm and rhyme of "Lover's Island" made everyone want to dance close to someone special. I took Esther's soft hand as we stood and began to dance, safe in each other's arms.

"Hey, what's happening? Robert, look." I pointed to the entrance where Mr. West was poised, speaking to someone unseen at the door that had been left open to circulate fresh air.

"I don't know. Let's find out."

As we approached, I saw Smiley Loco's face leaning forward over the arm that Mr. West braced across the doorway to prevent his entry.

"Look, Smiley, we don't want any trouble tonight," said Mr. West, barely moving his lips.

"Hey, man, *I* don't want any trouble tonight," Smiley replied slowly in drunken, slurred words. "I just want to dance. I got money and I got my woman. So let me in."

"And who are they?" Mr. West glared at the '51 Chevy that was parked nearby, filled with the shadow forms of his gang.

"Hey, man, they are here to make sure I get in." Smiley Loco chuckled in a low hoarse tone and nodded his head toward the car. On signal, his gang poured out of the car with their hands in their coat pockets as two other cars pulled up.

"You're not welcome. Get out of here before I call the cops!" Mr. West slammed the door shut.

The music stopped. I felt Big Toben and Speedo brush past me and the small ring of people who had gathered to watch the argument.

"Let us out!" yelled Big Toben as he shot a hard stare into Mr. West's eyes. From outside a loud, wild pounding against the door began.

"No!" Mr. West answered stiffly as he held onto the door handle. "No one is leaving until I say so!"

"Look, we can take care of them!" Big Toben was now

surrounded by his gang, each waiting for the word to crash through the door.

Mr. West braced his shoulder against the door as the noise from outside increased and the blows on the door threatened to break through.

"No one leaves the dance! You gave me your word, Big Toben, remember?" Mr. West looked frantic, desperate. "Are you man enough to keep it?"

With the loud banging outside, the fiery stares between Mr. West and Big Toben were broken when Big Toben rolled his eyes to the ceiling and smiled.

"I'll keep my word." Big Toben relaxed his body and stepped back slowly. "I said I wouldn't go out those doors until the dance is over, and I won't." He turned his back to Mr. West and faced his gang. "Let's go through the windows to the roof!"

The crowd followed Big Toben as he ran to the far wall, pushing and stacking tables and chairs into a pyramid to climb through a transom window that led to the roof.

"Wait!" Mr. West couldn't do anything but hold onto the door handle and brace himself against the loud banging from outside. "Miss Johnson, please call the police!"

"See those cases of empty Coke bottles?" Big Toben signaled to me. "Let's get them on the roof. We can use them!"

Once on the roof, we looked over the edge of the building. Below we saw the Eastside gang taking turns slamming the door with tire irons and chains while Smiley Loco, holding his girl around her waist, grinned through the side of his crooked mouth.

"Each of you take a good supply of bottles and wait till I give the word," said Big Toben.

Below in the gym, the girls, who had formed a supply line, passed as many Coke bottles as possible to the roof.

"Hey, Smiley!" echoed Big Toben from above. "Up here, Smiley!"

Smiley's grin faded as all eyes below looked up. Then the Eastside gang slowly stepped back toward their Chevy.

"This is my barrio and I want you to stay out!" shouted Big Toben. "Here!" He rifled a Coke bottle at Smiley who let go of his girlfriend and ran for cover.

Now all the Arroyo boys stood up and threw Coke bottles down on the Eastside gang as they ran to their cars. The hail of bottles shattered on the pavement below, spraying glass knives in all directions as Eastside shielded their heads and eyes.

When Eastside reached their cars, the storm of bottles exploded onto the car tops, denting hoods and fenders and shattering windshields.

I watched the cars from the roof as the engines started up and slowly rolled away over the broken glass. Everyone turned to Big Toben, who threw the last bottle as the cars now raced down the driveway onto the street.

"All right!" shouted Big Toben, standing with his fist clenched above his head.

BLAM! A noise from the parking lot echoed through the night. Big Toben dropped to the roof like a bird shot in flight. Everyone else fell to their stomachs in a heartbeat.

"What the hell was that?" Big Toben was lying on his side, holding his right hand to his head. "I felt something zing past."

"I don't know. It sounded like a car backfired," I said. "Or a gunshot."

Police sirens screamed faintly in the distance.

Walking back and forth in my backyard, like a cooped pigeon looking for a way out, I wished I could talk to Dad about Big Toben, Smiley Loco, and the gangs. I needed his advice. I remembered Mr. West's and Miss Johnson's warning, "Stay out of gangs, away from Big Toben!" But I felt I had to join him. Yet something nagged at me, too, like a teacher after a missing homework assignment.

Now standing in front of the empty coop, looking at it with regret, I felt that ever since I sold the pigeons, things were not right, like last night's close call with a bullet.

We needed the money, though. I didn't have a choice. I had to sell them. Okay, maybe there was another way, but I made the decision. I took care of things for my family. It's what Dad would have done.

Then I noticed pigeons, my pigeons landing on the coop—first singles, then in pairs, now in threes and fours, until most of my pigeons were back, perched in front of me.

"Why'd you come back? You can't stay here. Mr. García owns you now," I shouted. "Go on. What's done is done. Go back to Mr. García." I threw my hands up in the air, trying to scare them; the pigeons only re-tucked their wings, hopped, and resettled.

"Get out of here." I felt a hot surge of shame and anger flood my face. I rattled the doors of the coop and, when that didn't scare them, I swept my hand across their breasts, chasing them into the air, but only for a few moments. The birds found their perch again, unafraid.

I did the right thing. I made the best decision I knew how. I ran into the house to my room, sudden hot tears running down my cheeks. I threw myself down on my bed. The tears kept coming out against my will, and I felt weak. After a while the soft coo-cooing of the pigeons outside put me to sleep.

Later that night I woke up to find my brother, Henry, standing on top of my headboard, looking out the window that opened over the front doorsteps.

"Go to bed, Henry," I said, watching his stiff body on tiptoes, hands gripping like claws to the windowsill, and a corner of his wide eye looking out from under the curtain that covered his head like grandma's shawl. "What's wrong? What are you looking at?"

"There's an old man out there sitting on the steps," Henry said, calmly turning his eyes to me. "He's wearing a gray trucker's uniform, like Dad's."

"It's okay. It's all right," I said as I got out of my bed, brought Henry down from the window and tucked him under the covers. "Go to sleep. Everything's okay."

Then I pulled the curtain to one side and looked out the window at a dark, empty, cement-gray doorstep that held no answers, but was a place where my father had often sat late at night, long after everyone had gone to sleep.

CHAPTER 8

"Devil or Angel"

—The Clovers

At to Big Toben's house, I followed a smiling Esther to the bedroom where Big Toben sat at the edge of his bed looking at the black leather shoe he had in his hand. He looked at it like a jeweler would a diamond. I could tell that he had worked on it for hours; the shoe shone with a black, hard, deep gloss that reflected Big Toben's face when he looked into it.

"The left shoe always seems the hardest to get to a shine," Big Toben said, smiling at me.

"Yeah, I know," I said as I sat in a chair next to the bed. I watched Big Toben as he held the corner of an old diaper around his index finger, twisting it tightly. Then he wet his covered finger in a small drop of spit, dipped into the black Kiwi Shoe Wax and rubbed a small dot of it onto the toe of the shoe. He worked slowly and carefully until the creamy wax went deep and came to a mirror finish.

"Smiley Loco was surprised last night, eh, man?" Big Toben said, putting his shoe down and setting up the ironing board. His attention was now directed at ironing his clothes.

"Yeah, it was wild," I said. "They say he has a shotgun. Do you think he used it last night?"

"Probably," Big Toben replied, setting up the iron. I watched Big Toben's wet fingertip sizzle as he tested the heat of the iron. Then he stretched his beige khakis across the ironing board, folding one leg on top of the other so that he could make a knife-thin crease. He laid a damp diaper over the pant leg to get a hot, steamy press. After the pants were pressed, like two stiff boards, he made a one-fourth-inch cuff on each leg and pressed it in place. Next, he placed his "Sir Guy" Pendleton shirt on the ironing board and began to steam in the military pleats, three in back, two in front.

"Were you scared?" I asked, looking up at the ceiling as I stroked the "peach fuzz" on my chin.

"Yeah, but what difference does it make?" Big Toben said, placing his shirt on a hanger. "When your time comes, it comes. There's nothing you can do about it."

I was quiet, trying to understand.

"See that picture over there?" Big Toben said, pointing to the opposite wall. There I saw a paper print of an Aztec Indian warrior and an Indian maiden. The strong warrior stood straight and tall, aiming an arrow high into the sky. A leather headdress of short red, green, blue, and yellow feathers covered his long black hair. His head was turned to the left, showing the right side of his brown face and a small earring of gold. He wore a *tigre* skin across his broad shoulders, a thick loincloth of spun maguey strands and strong sandals of soft deer skin. His bronze skin glowed, showing off his bulging chest muscles and the swelled veins of his flexed arms and legs. His proud body was against a backdrop of eerie gray clouds that covered a black sky.

Lying by his feet was a young woman in a white dress. Brightly colored embroideries edged the dress that showed her silhouette. Her dark nipples were visible through the thin cloth. She was barefooted and wore no jewelry. A circle of small pink flowers crowned her jet-black hair.

"When I was younger my mother often told me about the legend of the warrior and maiden," Big Toben said. "Do you want to hear it?"

"Yeah, sure," I said.

Big Toben began to tell the story:

"The warrior was from the tribe called the 'Dog People' and was considered unworthy of the beautiful Aztec princess. He loved her and she loved him but her father, the Aztec king, wouldn't let them marry. After a long time, the warrior proved himself by surviving the many trials of strength and courage the king gave him before he could win the princess. Finally, he was given the maiden to be his wife. On the wedding day the bride-to-be climbed alone to a high mountain peak. This was the custom of the Aztec people. There she sought purity through solitude and nearness to the sky, the home of the gods. She wanted to get a true blessing, and so she chose to climb one of the highest mountains that surrounded the Valley of Mexico where she lived. But the distance to the top was so far, she was beaten down by the heat of the Sun, the god of time. When she did not return at the expected hour, the warrior became worried. But tribal custom would not let him climb the mountain to search for her. *De veras*, no one could go to her. Everyone was bound by tradition to honor her loneliness, no matter how long it took. But the warrior climbed the mountain to get his princess anyway. When he found her, she was lying at the top of the mountain looking like she was asleep under a blazing sun. But the sun had killed her. The warrior stood over her body, shaded her, trying to save her. Then, after taking an arrow from the leather holder strapped to his shoulder, he pulled back his bow with all his strength and shot an arrow at the far away sun. But the warrior was helpless against the sun, against time."

When he finished, Big Toben took a drag on his cigarette without taking his eyes from the picture.

Later that evening the sweet Ripple wine was passed from the driver, Poison, 18, to Speedo, then to the back seat where Big Toben and I sat. We were coming from cruising Whittier Boulevard in Eastside, driving in Toben's 1950 midnight blue Ford that floated inches above the pavement with green glowing lights underneath the fenders. On the right rear window "Lover's Island" was printed in Old English script.

"The cops," Poison whispered, as he looked at the red light reflected in his rearview mirror. "Throw that stuff out the window." Poison stomped the gas pedal to the floorboard.

"What are you doing?" I asked.

"He's gonna have to catch us first, man."

The Ford streaked down Vine Street, heading for the freeway with the black and white close behind, siren blaring.

I was silent. Poison turned down the narrow street that runs along the freeway going east. He made the turn at top speed, foot to the floorboard, while Speedo pressed on the brake pedal with all his strength. The car made the turn sideways on two wheels, squealing. I thought that if we could get back to our territory, Big Arroyo, we would have a better chance of losing the cops.

Poison made another last minute turn. The sudden jerk of the car threw open the right rear door, and sent me and Big Toben flying out. I fell onto the ground as the car sped on. I looked around and realized that I was alone in the "Fields." Mr. Yashita's roses grew tall and sweet in the dark. Big Toben was nowhere in sight. I slowly crawled along the rows of rose bushes dodging the police spotlights shining from the street. When I reached the other side of the field, my shirt in shreds, my skin scratched and caked with blood, I ran through the park to my house.

At home I silently peeked in and watched my mother in her room kneeling before her statues of Jesus and Mary. A lone candle flickered before the images, causing their shadows to dance on the walls and ceiling. My mother had her head bowed and her long hair covered her face like a black curtain. As she slowly patted her fist to her heart, I heard her whisper:

"*Por mi culpa, por mi culpa, por mi gravísima culpa . . .*"

I watched as she took the rosary beads from the neck of the clay Virgin. She worked the beads with her left hand because her right index finger was all bandaged up.

The white gauze and tape reminded me of her accident. It happened two weeks ago when she brought sewing home from the factory. My mother was sewing garments as quickly as possible so that she could earn a good wage for piece work. I remembered that she was very tired at the end of the day and that's when it happened. As she pushed a burlap hem underneath the three-inch steel needle, it shot into her finger again and again, ripping her skin and cracking her bone until the needle broke. The broken metal stayed stuck in her finger as the machine came to a stop.

"I won't scream. I won't scream," she whispered to herself as tears fell from her cheeks into the growing rings of blood. Bringing her torn finger to her mouth, she jerked the broken needle free with her teeth.

"It's my fault," she said to me as I came running to help.

Now in her darkened room as I watched, she looked at her bandaged wound and, holding it before the flame, said, "*Por mi culpa, por mi culpa, por mi gravísima culpa . . .*"

CHAPTER 9

"All I Have to Do Is Dream"
—The Everly Brothers

I sat in the corner next to the window. Looking at Miss Johnson, standing so straight and tall at the front of the room, I wondered if everything she said was true. Did she really sleep with a hardwood board underneath her mattress? She looked the way I thought Abe Lincoln looked, tall and thin. An Abe Lincoln in a dress. She was queen-like and almost mysterious. I felt like she could look at me and know everything that was going on in my head.

"How many of you have heard of Will Rogers?" asked Miss Johnson, my ninth-grade English teacher.

No one raised their hand. I watched as spokes of light came through the window blinds and lighted narrow pathways of dust into the room. The hardwood floors shined. The warm air was filled with the smell of floor wax and pomade.

"My word. Well, he was an important man in the recent history of America. He was a humorist when America needed humor most. During the Depression, he . . ." She began to pace the room now as she talked about oil fields, poverty, and the rise of union labor.

"I never met a man I didn't like," quoted Miss Johnson, wearing her short white hair like a crown.

I was sitting across the room when I heard Little Martin, a runty clown, loudly clearing his throat. When I turned to look, Martin held two purple tablets up for me to see. I smiled. I knew that the tablets, a candy called Fizzies, foamed when dropped into water to make a sugary drink.

". . . the only nation in the world that went to the poor house in an automobile," quoted Miss Johnson, smiling alone.

Little Martin slipped the tablets into his mouth, slumped in his chair and began to moan. Purple foam oozed from the corners of his mouth and he began to shake.

"What's wrong with you?" asked Miss Johnson, walking toward him. Martin only groaned and made a trail of bubbles come out of his mouth over his purple lips.

"Everyone outside! Outside!" said Miss Johnson as she leaned over and held Little Martin by the shoulders and watched as his eyes rolled back.

Robert and I led the students out into the main hallway and through the double doors into the sun. I heard everyone laughing as we took off in all directions, past the brown dirt softball diamond to the grassy football field near Temple Avenue.

"Don't forget the game with Big Arroyo Saturday," I said. I was sitting on the thirty-yard line picking blades of grass and putting them into my mouth while my buddies sat in a ring near me. "What do you think will happen to Martin?"

"She'll send Martin home after they ask him, 'Why did you do it?'" answered Robert as Pete and DeSoto, sitting next to me nodded their heads. Pete was a muscular sort, man-boy with long black hair combed back. His face was scarred by acne. DeSoto, who was short and round, often drove his father's car, a DeSoto.

"And you two will be blamed for it," Pete said, looking at Robert and me. "What's she going to say to you two anyway?"

"Well, let's see," I went on. "She'll say, 'Why did you boys put him up to it?' And we'll say that we didn't put anybody up to anything and she'll go, 'You boys know you should set an example for the rest of the school. Now what made you boys put Martin up to such a thing?' And we'll say . . ." I turned my head toward the sound of a police siren a few blocks away. Then everyone looked. We could see someone running toward us, about a block away. As the guy in a T-shirt and Khaki pants grew larger, I recognized him. It was Big Toben, running like a rolling tumbleweed, arms pumping and his head bobbing like a cork at the end of a fishing line.

As the siren grew louder, I was thinking that maybe the police were finishing last night's chase. So I was the first to stand up, waiting for Big Toben to come near.

Now, about five yards away, Big Toben paid no attention to our nervous stares. He climbed the chain-link fence, and jumped to the ground on our side.

"You didn't see nobody!" shouted Big Toben, out of breath as a black and white, siren blaring, turned the corner only a few yards away. Big Toben stared across the open field that had no hiding places, and he started to run.

"Big Toben, wait!" I yelled. "Miss Johnson is coming. If the cops don't see you, she will." I pointed to Miss Johnson who was just now leaving the double doors of the school building, heading our way.

"Here, huddle in with us and we'll walk together as one group toward her with you in the middle." I led all the boys as we got around Big Toben, and then moved together toward Miss Johnson who was now blowing on a whistle and waving for everyone to come in.

"Hey, all of you, stop!" The screeching tires and slamming car doors let us know the cops had arrived.

"What? Huh? We gotta go, officer. Here comes Miss Johnson."

I led the others into a slow trot toward Miss Johnson who now saw the cops standing near the fence. One of them waved his hand and then they sped off.

When we reached the door, Big Toben went around the building, while the rest of us motioned for Miss Johnson to go ahead of us into the building and the empty classroom.

"Now I've called you boys in here because I want to talk to you about Martin and this last disagreeable episode," said Miss Johnson, looking at us from behind her desk where a dictionary and a thick book with the title, "The Life of Will Rogers" sat between stone bookends.

Looking bored, Robert sat closest to her. As I watched, Robert slowly took a needle and thread from his leather belt and began sewing the top layer of skin on the palm of his hand.

"You boys should set an example for the rest of the school," said Miss Johnson, appearing to ignore Robert's careful stitching. "Robert, you have been elected the president of the graduating ninth grade class. That should mean something to you, but it doesn't and I know why. I know a lot about you both. For instance, Robert, you're a perfectionist. Things must be done exactly right. If not, you get very upset. You must learn that imperfection is the order of the day. Don't misunderstand me. You should continue to expect the best from yourself, but be fair to others. If you hold on to your convictions and learn to handle your disappointment in others, your future is promising."

Robert pulled the thread through the skin in his hand until it came free. He returned the threaded needle to his belt and folded his arms across his chest, keeping his eyes down.

"Now, David, you've changed considerably since last year when the only thing you were concerned with was your pet pigeons and studying. You were at the top of your class. But now, well . . . I think I understand what's been happening, though. You're breaking out of your shell. You're as much an introvert as Robert is an extrovert. Do you know what I mean? You used to keep to yourself. You were very shy. But now you're growing out of it. That's what I mean about breaking out of your shell. Now I hope both of you see that I'm trying to understand what you're going through. I realize that . . ."

I was looking at her while she was talking. I felt like she had turned me inside out. I was embarrassed, burning red from head to foot.

". . . and I saw what happened just now on the playing field." Miss Johnson's serious, almost gloomy voice got my attention. "You shielded Big Toben from the police. You helped him elude them. I don't think that was right."

At that, I cracked my knuckles loudly and gave her a dirty look.

"I know you don't like to be preached to," she leaned forward over her clasped hands, "but I can't help feeling that there is something better for you than to follow in Big Toben's footsteps."

"Can we go now?" I asked, turning my head away from her and sighing as if bored to tears.

"Yes. I suppose so," answered Miss Johnson, not one to give up easily. "One day you both are going to have to make a choice."

With that Robert and I rose and started to walk out of the room.

"David," called Miss Johnson, "I'm submitting your essay to the Stanford Scholastic Contest. I think you have a good chance of garnering a scholarship."

"What essay?" Robert asked once we were outside. I shrugged my shoulders.

"Oh, I guess the writing assignment I turned in two days ago," I said. I really didn't want anyone to know.

"She never gives up, does she?" Robert shook his head.

CHAPTER 10

"Cucurrucucú, Paloma"

—Tomás Méndez

At the dinner table everyone sat waiting as our mother brought large bowls of *menudo* for everyone, including Robert who sat next to Rosie. Rosie stole shy glances at Robert whenever she got a chance. Once the steaming bowls were set in front of us, the small cups of diced onions and chopped cilantro were passed along so that each person could drop a pinch into their *menudo*. I put the freshly ground oregano into my bowl and began eating as mother set a stack of warm tortillas in the middle of the table.

After dinner everyone got ready to watch wrestling on TV. I adjusted the television set just like my father had always done on Thursday nights. I had everyone sit around on the floor near the couch. In the kitchen, mother was popping popcorn.

"Someone's at the door," Rosie said as our sisters brought pillows and blankets to curl up with as they watched. I was busy moving the rabbit-ear antennas.

Rosie went to the door, opened it, and I saw Uncle Rico,

El Cuate, standing there. I could see he looked worn out, standing in the doorway, not saying a word.

"It's Uncle Rico," called Rosie. "Hi, Uncle, come in."

Uncle Rico walked in, grinning, his steps heavy on the floor and his bullet-hole eyes sunken deep into his brown face.

"Uncle Rico, come in," I said. "Are you going to watch wrestling with us tonight?"

I knew that Uncle Rico was not quite right in the head ever since his twin brother died. Los Cuates were my father's youngest brothers. When they were young they were the center of attention, like family celebrities. Mike and Rico were always together. Mike was the quiet, shy one, and Rico the loud joker. They were opposites. Mike always protected Rico. Rico always pulled practical jokes on Mike, but Mike never got angry. He took all of Rico's pranks with a smile. Once Rico pretended to be Mike and took Mike's date out for a night on the town in Mike's car. The girl never knew the difference. When Mike found out he only laughed and said, "That's my brother, always fooling around."

They were identical twins. Actually the mirror image of each other, handsome as movie stars. Six-feet-tall, thin, muscular bodies with faces that stopped women in the streets. My mother said it was their brown, fine features, small, bedroom eyes, outlined by black eyebrows and long eyelashes that women couldn't resist. Their smiles revealed straight white teeth. Each had a small mole on his cheek. Mike's sat on his left just above his jaw and Rico's was the same except on the opposite side, so that when they stood facing each other, it really was a mirror image.

When Mike enlisted to fight in the Korean War, Rico didn't want to go along. He told everybody he had "flat feet" or something. Besides, he joked that he was the man that was going to keep all the lonely girls company now that all the boys had gone to war.

But when the news came home that Mike was killed in action, Rico became very sad, he tried to kill himself, and sometimes he became very violent. At family gatherings, police were often needed to get him under control. Things only got worse for Rico, and doctors had to give him shock treatments to help him with his sadness and aggression.

"Sit here, Uncle Rico," I said. "In Dad's chair."

Rico sat down slowly, closing his eyes and breathing deeply as he rested in the worn recliner.

I sat beside Robert on the couch opposite the TV screen. Rosie squeezed in next to Robert.

"The wrestling matches are almost on," I said, knowing that everyone was anxious for the match to begin. "Hey, while we're waiting, I'll arm wrestle Robert. Uncle Rico, you be the referee."

Rico opened his eyes, nodded, and pulled back the sleeve of his shirt and showed his big muscles, but didn't move from the chair.

Robert and I put our elbows on the coffee table and began to push, grunt, and groan as the others watched. Seeing our faces turn chili red, Uncle Rico jumped out of his chair, shouting and pointing, "Look over there!"

When everyone turned to look, Uncle Rico pulled our clenched hands apart and slammed them both to the table.

"I won," said Uncle Rico as the girls laughed at his trick.

"Can we have a glass of water, too?" asked Barbara when the bowls of popcorn came.

"Sure, you can," I said. I knew that the girls were testing our father's superstitious belief that drinking water after eating popcorn would give a person a very bad stomach ache. He said it could only be cured by a pot full of boiled *yerba buena* from the garden.

As everyone got in position to watch the wrestling matches, I adjusted the rabbit ears one more time.

Tonight's card included Gorgeous George, Antonio Argentina Rocca, Mr. Moto, Primo Carnera, and the Masked Marvel.

The show began with the announcer in the middle of the ring shouting the arrival of Gorgeous George, who was led in by his butler, Jefferies. Jefferies wore white gloves and carried a gold tray holding bobby pins, a perfume bottle, and disinfectant spray into the ring. He put the tray on the ring apron and laid out a red and purple rug in the corner for the "Gorgeous One" to step on. Then from the back of the arena, Gorgeous George made his grand entrance under a bright spotlight with palace guards and classical music. His red and gold robe made his long blonde curls of hair stand out. When he got close to the ring, the Gorgeous One was met by Jefferies who held the ropes apart and helped his master to the center of the mat. Then Jefferies sprayed perfume on Gorgeous George's robe and hair.

The match itself was not much to see, not much action, with Gorgeous George taking the first fall in 10:22 minutes.

I elbowed Robert to get his attention. I pointed to the chair where Uncle Rico sat snoring, deep in sleep.

The next match was a brutal one. Huge Primo Carnera, a former world's heavyweight boxing champion, stomped into the ring and grabbed the other wrestler by his shoulders and neck. He used his strength to break an armlock by throwing the other guy into the ropes. But the wrestler bounced off the ropes and met "Da Preem" head on and both went, weak-kneed, down to the canvas. Carnera just rolled over on top of the knocked out body to win the fall. The match continued with head butts, drop-kicks, and body slams.

By then all the popcorn had been eaten and the little kids were asleep in their warm blankets.

Uncle Rico woke up a while later and walked out the front door without saying a word.

Robert soon followed, leaving me to wake Rosie and Henry. I carried my little sisters to bed. Then I went back to the living room alone and sat in my father's chair, feeling the lumps and sags that had come from my father's daily use. I could almost smell my father's sweat and tobacco coming from the worn upholstery. My fingers tried to touch something more. I dug deep until my fingertips ached. Then I got up, turned the television off, and went to bed.

CHAPTER 11

"Love Potion #9"

—The Clovers

I noticed how she had a way of lowering her chin and focusing her eyes over the entire class, like a towering lighthouse I'd seen in a magazine once, shooting white beams of light over a foggy coast, making everything clear, at least for a while.

"You're not too young to start obtaining a world view," said Miss Johnson, holding her hands in front of her as she stood straight and tall at the head of the class near my desk. "That is, it's important for you to understand that what happens in other parts of the world *does* affect our country, the United States. Therefore, affects each and every one of you."

"For example," continued Miss Johnson, "a little country called Vietnam in the Far East could be considered a tinder box. The strife there could be the fuel that ignites another world war."

She talked about things that really mattered, I thought as I leaned up close to her, not wanting to miss a word.

"Can you show us that Viet . . . a . . . a, country on the map, please, Miss Johnson?" asked Martin, holding up his hand in the back of the room.

"Certainly," replied Miss Johnson as she stepped backwards, reaching high for the map ring and pulling it down. After squeakily unrolling the map, Miss Johnson, facing the class, pointed to the belly button of a nude Playboy magazine centerfold that was scotch-taped to the continents of the world. Hearing everyone's giggles and ahs, Miss Johnson turned, saw the picture, and snapped the map shut with a bang, bringing everyone to stone silence.

At the party that night, everyone paired up as they came through the door into María's living room. The girls had planned well, I thought. All the boys were happy with their partners, except me. I sat alone near the punch bowl watching Lesley, an eighteen-year-old high school girl who was the party's only chaperone. She wore a tight brown skirt that came down near her ankles, and a white cotton blouse, unbuttoned three down. She smiled. After a couple of glasses of spiked punch, I smiled back at her from across the room. To me she seemed to have a glow around her, like the girl on the TV soap commercial. She held a small glass cup of punch with one finger around the mermaid handle. Every now and then, she drank it, like a sea bird, hardly sipping. But when she had drunk it all, she fished for the ice cubes with her pink tongue. I smiled now whenever our eyes met; she smiled back.

My mind was made up. I wanted to dance with her. Now or never, I thought. I straightened my collar, ran my palm against my hair as I got up, walked to the punch bowl, and refilled my glass. I was relieved to sit down again. No, no, not yet, the next time I get up, I'll ask her to dance. After slowly finishing my punch, I walked across the room as casually as I could but nervous and out of breath. When I got near her, two girls huddled close to talk to her and blocked my way. It's too late to turn around, I decided. So I waited. I cleared my throat. I brushed my palm against my hair, pressing it into place. My eyes caught hers. She's so beautiful, I thought. Next I felt everybody's eyes on me. The girls had turned around to face me. Drops of sweat the size of avocados grew on my forehead. The room was silent. The music had stopped.

"Do you . . .," I whispered.

"Yes, a slow dance? You're the first person to ask me. Thank you," said Lesley, as she put her cup down.

When the music began, I took her hand and led her out to the dance floor. I held her at a distance like a full glass of milk until she pulled me close to her and put her hand underneath my shirt collar, squeezing the back of my neck with her fingers.

"This is the way I dance," she said.

As we danced, her warm body, sweet perfume, starched cotton blouse, and fuzzy wool skirt worked against me. As the music was about to end, I realized that I couldn't step away from her without everyone seeing how excited I really was. But when the music stopped, someone called to her and she walked away, thanking me as she left me alone in the middle of the dance floor. I put my hand in my front pocket and walked stiffly to my chair, watching the other boys nod and stare. I stayed there for about twenty minutes, staring at the floor. When I knew it was safe, I stood up and walked out the door.

Outside I felt the brisk wind chill my warm, flushed face. What happened in there? I couldn't help it. It just happened. I remembered the times in class when the teacher called on a boy to stand and answer a question when it was most inconvenient. As I walked along the sidewalk, I saw two people in the dark near the wall that bordered María's house.

"Why are you out here?" asked Robert as I got nearer. He was with Rhonda.

"No reason. Hey, Robert, are you too busy or can we finish the work we planned?"

"Work? Oh, yeah, right. Work," replied Robert as he pushed Rhonda toward the house. "Go inside. I'll be there in a minute, okay? See ya, later." Rhonda slowly dropped Robert's hand, but not until she tickled his palm with her finger . . . a promise of what was to come.

When she was inside, Robert got a spray paint can from his pocket and began writing, "Los Cuates de Oro, Arroyo Chico," our tag. As I watched, I listened to the rhythm of slow music, Fats Domino, coming from the darkened windows of María's house. When Robert finished the writing, we stood back to look at the large wavy script that showed well on the gray block wall.

"Watch out! Here comes a car," I cautioned, hearing a low rumbling from the street.

"It's Eastside!" Robert tossed the spray can over the fence.

"Hey, man, where you from?" called a voice from the slow moving car.

"Who wants to know?"

"I said, where you from, punk!" The car stopped. It was a '51 Chevy with wide, white side-wall tires and baby moon hubcaps that reflected light from the street lamps.

"I said who wants to know?"

I watched the car doors open slowly. A half-smirking Smiley Loco and three of his gang members in dark trench coats stepped out. A fourth member stayed behind the wheel of the running car. When they circled Robert and me, we turned back-to-back, ready to fight. I watched helplessly as a skinny guy with a flattop haircut moved over to the wall and sprayed "Eastside" in black paint across our tag.

"Los Cuates de Oro from Arroyo Chico are gonna die tonight." Smiley Loco pulled a hooked carpet knife from his inside coat pocket. I noticed that his ear was gone, except for a small ragged piece of earlobe that he pierced with a gold earring. Now the others pulled out their weapons: a chain, a tire iron and a metal pipe.

Robert and I crouched to the right in a small circle, touching butt-to-butt, as the four attackers moved around us, looking for an opening. I remembered all the rough play fighting and shadow boxing with my gang friends that got me ready for this. I felt strong with a back-up, but I was afraid, afraid that they might smell my fear. So I decided to strike first. I chose the tall one with the chain, but my eyes squeezed shut with the sharp pain of a strong, bright beam of light shining from the darkness.

"The cops!" yelled Smiley Loco, turning away and running to the car. The others followed, leaving Robert and me alone in the ring of light.

Holding my arm up to shade my eyes, I could see where the bright light was coming from. It was the spotlight of a 1950 Ford with Big Toben in the front seat.

The Eastside gang had barely pulled their doors closed when Big Toben's Ford rammed their Chevy in the rear, causing the chrome bumper to fall off into the street and the dented trunk lid to spring open.

"Here's for Eastside," shouted Big Toben as the Big Arroyo gang threw bricks, bottles, and tire irons at the Chevy. It screeched away, leaving behind shattered glass and the smell of burning tires.

"Hey, man," called Big Toben from the Ford as the spotlight focused on Robert and me. "You all right?"

"Yeah," Robert said.

"Yeah." I was relieved.

"Hey, man, I wouldn't want you two to get hurt before

the football game!" A burst of laughter echoed in the street as Big Toben and his gang cruised slowly away.

"I had a close call tonight. If it wasn't for Big Toben, Smiley Loco and his gang would have knifed us. Things are getting just like Mr. West warned, but I don't know what to do about it." I spoke to the empty pigeon coop in my backyard. "I can't drop out of the gang. There's loyalty . . . but I just feel like something bad will happen if the gangs keep going at each other like this. I've got to watch out."

I turned from the silence of the empty coop and went to bed. Later I heard the soft coo-coooing of pigeons as I lay in bed trying to sleep, or maybe to dream.

CHAPTER 12

"Yakety-Yak"

—The Coasters

"Have you two apologized to Miss Johnson yet?" Mr. West sat behind his desk across from me and Robert.

"No," said Robert, cocking his head to the right and letting a half smile break lose from the corner of his mouth like a puff of smoke.

"No," I answered in a slow whisper.

"And why not?" Mr. West leaned back in his chair, clasping his hands behind his head, driving his question deep into Robert's eyes with a hard stare. Robert didn't want to answer so he silently wiped the back of his hand across his mouth.

"You said it should be sincere, that we should really mean it," I said, looking at the desktop.

"Well, I understand, but I didn't call you here to talk about that," Mr. West said, leaning forward with his arms on the desk. "The problem is this: After the episode with the Playboy Bunny and the map, the principal feels there should be some severe disciplinary action."

"We didn't do anything!" Robert shot back.

"He thinks both of you and Martin should be suspended for three days." Mr. West looked at the blank wall across the room.

"But we didn't do anything!" Robert's back straightened as he leaned into Mr. West's view.

"You're not listening to me," Mr. West's voice grew deep and strong. "We're beyond that. This is the last straw. Do you know what I mean?"

"Why do we get blamed for everything everyone else does?" Robert crossed his arms on his chest.

"We didn't have anything to do with Martin taping the picture on the map. It was all his idea," I explained, trying to save something.

"You may not have told him to do it, but he does it because of you two. He wants to impress you," said Mr. West.

"Why's that our problem?" Robert spoke in a slow, careful way.

"It is."

I looked away, lost.

"You are the leaders," said Mr. West after a few minutes when he recovered his purpose. "You should know when the fun ends and the seriousness begins."

"We're always getting blamed for what others do, and that's not fair," I said.

"Fair or not, the others look up to both of you. You've got to set an example. These pranks must end. You're both smart enough to know that this fooling around can get serious very quickly and that's what we're trying to avoid." Mr. West appeared to feel he was gaining ground, connecting, reaching us. "For instance, you play tackle football without equipment just for 'kicks,' the thrill of it, but one of these days someone's going to get hurt, seriously hurt."

Robert hung his head and shook it, right to left, as if saying, "No."

"Why are you shaking your head?" asked Mr. West, showing anger.

"You don't understand," Robert said with bitterness.

No one spoke for a few minutes. It was a guarded silence, like the quiet before opening a letter that you know has bad news.

"Okay, look," Mr. West said, as if he felt this to be his final try. "I know it's hard being without fathers—"

"I've got a father!" Robert shouted, now standing, his rock fists at his sides, nostrils shaking, and his hard, black eyes stripping the air out of the room. After a few moments, he turned and stomped out.

"Wait," Mr. West called, stopping me as I started to follow Robert. "Give me a few more minutes, okay?"

I sat down again and waited.

"Look, I think you're headed in a direction that's not good for you—gangs and . . ." Mr. West tried to look into my downcast eyes.

I rose slowly from my chair.

"You must decide things for yourself, starting now.

Think about tomorrow, your future. You have to make a choice sometime."

I kept my head down as I moved toward the door.

"You have to start seeing what's really out there. You have to look the world square in the eye."

When I heard this, I stopped and turned to face him. His words seemed to be some kind of code that had meaning, the way grownups sometimes talk that I couldn't understand.

"Yes, look the world square in the eye."

"Can I go now?" I asked, needing to escape.

"Yes. Just one thing. I'm sorry if I offended Robert. Let him know that."

"Okay."

"Oh, wait a minute. Here's two gallons of white paint. Mrs. Torres says that her fence was vandalized the night of the party and needs painting. I told her that you two wouldn't mind doing it."

At home, feeling tired and hungry, I was grateful for the dinner my mother had made for me. The homey fragrance of *chile verde*, Spanish rice, and fresh flour tortillas filled my lungs as I thanked my mother and sat down to eat.

After dinner, I climbed onto the roof, lay on my back, and let the dry, warm Santa Ana winds roll over me. The stiff breezes blew as I stared above into the bowl of blackness that held floating eyes of light. In the distance, a steady coo-cooing of pigeons, like a distant alarm clock, brought me back from the sky and the stars.

I thought about the pigeons. I felt strangely like them as they played out their lives. Here in Little Arroyo, I felt happy, safe. Maybe, I thought, to be safe inside the barrio with my friends, to play Saturday football, to take care of my mother, and protect the territory was enough. What was wrong with that? West and Johnson were always nagging me about the future—about high school, even college. "Be somebody before it's too late!" Too late! Too late for what? They always talked in code, knowing everything, telling nothing.

I listened. The coo-cooing was broken by the soft echo of a gun going off somewhere in the barrio. Then another crack scared a nearby covey of pigeons to flight. I watched their ghostly, crooked shadows cross the silver moon.

Then I shook when I heard ambulance sirens crying somewhere in the streets of my barrio, reminding me of death.

CHAPTER 13

"Speedo"

—The Cadillacs

Saturday morning from my rooftop I saw tiny specks of white and brown gliding through the air—the pigeons in the distance and below. I looked over my barrio, laid out like a giant puzzle of shrubs, sidewalks, car tops, electric wires, and fences. Backyards were visible, like open closets, showing all the stuff that people didn't use anymore, but hid from the neighbors.

I was ready to play football. I looked past a dozen rooftops toward Arroyo Park. On the other side of the basketball court, I spotted the guys running across the grass. I climbed down from the roof and called Robert on the phone, then headed for the park. I knew that Big Toben and his gang would be waiting for us.

When we got to the park, I found all the Big Arroyo and Little Arroyo players sitting in separate circles on the grass with their shoes off. Others, side-by-side, stood on the broad blades of grass that caused their toes to dig. Some boys sprinted in bursts across the field trying to get the "feel of it." Others sat down and brought a grass stem to their mouths to chew, letting the rough underside stab at their lips. The sliced-watermelon smell of freshly cut grass filled our lungs. We were ready. It would be Shirts against Skins.

I wondered how my team, the Skins, would do. I knew our best player was the quarterback, Eddie, a thin, dark-skinned sixteen-year-old. He had a great passing arm and was good at calling plays. But the other team was older and bigger. They had a strong-armed quarterback who often warmed up before a game by throwing the football straight into the air, aiming at low-flying pigeons. But I knew that what my team lacked in size they gained in speed.

After the kick-off, we had the ball on the twenty-yard line. In the huddle, Eddie, on one knee, drew a play on the palm of his hand with his finger.

"Robert's right-half, you're left, DeSoto. David's right-end, Al left, Martin is center. The rest of you block. Now I'll get the ball on two, fake a hand off to the left-half coming straight into the line and give it to Robert sweeping left. Robert, when you get the ball, you run like a bat-outta-hell! On two." Eddie clapped his hands, sending everyone out of the huddle to their positions.

"Hut one, hut two," Eddie shouted, setting the play in motion. Big Arroyo took the fake, and Robert ran down the sideline, side-stepping one would-be tackler, and scored untouched.

A few plays later, Big Arroyo had the ball. Big Toben

played football without fear. Few players would even try to tackle him. He was big and fast on his feet. Most players were afraid a good tackle might make him mad. But Big Toben knew it and gave the other team a chance by blocking instead of running with the ball.

On the next play, I figured out Big Toben's plan was to get the smallest guy on his team, Tiny, to hold on to his belt while Big Toben led the way down the field. Tiny looked like a handkerchief in Big Toben's back pocket, blowing in the wind. Nothing could stop this rolling buffalo, except a tackle from behind.

Late in the game, with the score tied at twenty-one, I watched as Big Toben headed toward the end zone for a long pass. Robert was racing to the same spot for an interception. When both of them leapt high into the air to catch the ball, they crashed into each other. Big Toben, holding the ball, went flying into the wooden grape-stake fence that bordered the end zone. I heard a loud cracking sound as he went through the old, dry boards. Robert fell to the ground like a pile of dirty laundry. All the players came running.

Big Toben slowly freed himself from the splintered fence that lay all around him. With the football in one hand and a broken fence stake in the other, he looked mean. He walked over to Robert who was still testing weak legs. Robert looked scared as Big Toben stood only a few inches away from his face.

"Did I score?" asked Big Toben breathing heavily into Robert's face. Robert slowly nodded yes.

"All right!" yelled Big Toben, smiling. "Good hit, man!" He let the stick fall to the ground from his hand.

It was nearly dark when I stopped to count the football injuries. There were three bloody noses from elbows, one back injury caused by a clothes-line tackle, and two players still lying on the ground curled up like babies with their breath knocked out of them.

When we couldn't see the ball anymore, we walked from the field, tired and bloody. Big Arroyo had won, but when I shook Big Toben's hand, I felt closer to him than ever before.

"You guys played a good game." Big Toben smiled. "See you here next Saturday."

"Yeah," I said. "Oh, wait a minute. I just remembered, Mr. West planned a car wash for next Saturday. Both of us, together, Big and Little."

"Oh, yeah? That sounds good. We'll do it. Together. Big and Little Arroyo." Big Toben grew serious. "Together, that's the way it should be."

"All right," I shook his hand again. "Here's the case of beer. It's cold."

"Thanks, man," Big Toben said as he reached for the case. "You guys are all right!"

I followed Big Toben who carried the case of beer over to the members of his team squatting near a tree in a semi-circle, joking and laughing.

"Help yourselves." Big Toben dropped the case of beer next to them. "It's cold."

After a while, I lay on my back and looked up at the sky as it grew bright with stars and a full moon rising. As the others drank, their tiredness became silliness and the joking grew louder.

"Hey, anybody seen Smiley Loco's new car?" Poison asked. "He's got no bumper and there are these gray primer spots all over the place to hide the dents we made."

Everyone laughed.

"Well, now the car looks like him!" Poison continued. "You know with all those spots and funny rear end, it looks like a hyena." Poison positioned himself on his hands and knees, like a hyena, crouching and laughing with a Smiley Loco crooked-face.

Everyone exploded with laughter and threw their empty beer cans at the hyena, Smiley Loco, in fake anger.

"He's the kind of guy that gives us a bad name," Speedo said. "*Loco*, crazy. He has no brains. He'll do anything, even kill his own."

When all the beer cans were sucked dry, I lay on my side with my head propped in my hand, staring into the dark, shadowy trees and shrubs. I listened to the soft coo-cooing of pigeons somewhere high on a nearby telephone pole.

"Let's go cruising Eastside," Poison said. "Let's go check out the Hyena Loco."

"Yeah, all right," Speedo said.

"I've got to change clothes." Big Toben got to his feet and slowly turned toward his gang. "I'll walk home. Come on, David, go with me. Give us fifteen minutes, then come by my house and pick us up."

"Okay," Speedo agreed. "We'll kill time with a smoke-out."

I watched Big Toben give a "go-ahead" look, and four of the guys jumped into the 1950 Ford. I watched them as they rolled up all the windows and lit their cigarettes. It was a game of "chicken." I wondered who would be the first one to run out of the smoke-filled car, gasping for air. Probably Poison, I thought.

"Hey, remember," Big Toben turned to the others who were watching and waiting, "pick us up in fifteen minutes."

Tall maple trees with huge dry leaves that looked like my dad's old leather work gloves, lined the street toward Big Toben's house. As I kept up beside him, I felt proud to be on even terms with Big Toben, a leader, looked up to and listened to. We walked with long, even steps, and the silence between us felt good. I felt as if the very next word, or action, or sound that broke the silence would be Truth. I waited.

Then I heard the muffled rumble of a car engine and the sticky friction of tires against warm pavement. I became alert. I couldn't seem afraid or turn and look back. Big Toben and I would wait until the they were well ahead of us before taking a casual look.

Blam! An explosion ripped the air and just in front of us a small mound of dirt and grass blew upward at our feet. But we continued our slow steady walk without missing a beat.

Out of the corner of my eye, I could see the front end of a lowered '51 Chevy glide into view, carrying Smiley Loco and his gang from Eastside.

"*Gordo, Gordito*, you *panzón*," a voice called from the car as it kept up alongside us.

But we kept walking, looking straight ahead. The weight of silence returned, except for the soft churning of the slow-moving car and the crackling of dried leaves underneath our black polished leather shoes.

"Hey, Big Toben!" Smiley Loco called. I watched Big Toben turn and throw a mean stare into Smiley's dark, pitted face.

"*Gordo,* we come to collect," Smiley Loco said softly.

"You're early, man. The garbage cans don't get put out till Monday," Big Toben said as I watched Smiley Loco slowly turn his twisted face toward the back seat. The dark barrel of a sawed-off shotgun slid through the open back window and glinted in the streetlight. Then I felt Big Toben's powerful hands on my chest, shoving me to the ground. I watched as Big Toben turned, raised a finger, and shouted, "*Chinga* . . ."

The rifle barrel glowed red, and Big Toben flew into the air and fell down, bleeding and dying beside me as the car sped off.

CHAPTER 14

"What'd I Say"

—Ray Charles

"**D**on't cry," I said, entering my mother's room where she knelt beside her bed.

"I can't help it," she said. "I just think how it could have been you."

"Big Toben, he saved my life," I said as I sat on the bed next to her.

"I know," she said, looking down. "But for what? Another time?"

"What?" I tried to see into her eyes.

"I've heard that your gang and his gang plan to avenge his death." She looked into my face. "It's not right, David."

"Yes, it is," I jumped to my feet. "Smiley Loco doesn't deserve to live. We have to get him. I have to do it."

"No. Let the police do it," she begged. "Why don't you help them? They say you know more than you're telling them. That you know who shot Big Toben, but you won't tell them."

"But I don't," I said.

"Why are you lying to me?" Her voice was shaking, her heart broken with pain.

"I'm not lying, Mamá. I'm telling the truth. The gun came out of the window. Big Toben pushed me down. I couldn't see who pulled the trigger. Maybe it was Smiley. Maybe someone else. I don't know," I moaned.

"But your friends, your friends think you're a big man for not telling the police. Your friends don't know what you've told me?" She pulled me down to sit next to her on the bed, holding me around the shoulders.

"No. It doesn't matter," I said in short, even breaths. "I know what I have to do."

"But it's not right, *m'ijo*," she soothed. "When is this going to end—an eye for an eye. If your father was here . . ."

"Well, he's not. I am." I jumped to my feet and pounded my chest with a tightly closed fist. "I know what I have to do."

My mother reached up with her open hand. But I turned and walked away, sucking in hard the baby cries of pain that she must have heard even before I made them. I was both ashamed and angry at myself for showing a wound I thought was so well hidden.

Later, from my room, I heard a knock at the front door and my mother answering it.

"Hi, Mrs. López." I heard clearly through the open window. "I'm Mr. West. I'd like to talk to David, if it's all right?"

"Yes, I'll get him," she replied. "Come in, come in."

When I reached the living room where Mr. West sat, he

put his hand out for me to shake.

"I just wanted to see how you were doing," Mr. West said, his elbows resting on his knees.

"I'm okay." I sat in Dad's chair across from him. "I'm fine."

"Listen, I, I know it must be hard for you," Mr. West spoke softly. "Some very tragic events have occurred in a short period of time. If you need someone to talk to. If you're confused . . ."

"I'm not confused," I broke in. "I can handle it. I know what to do."

"And exactly what is that?" Mr. West seemed angry. "Well?"

"I know and that's enough."

"Revenge? Is that what you know?" Mr. West questioned. "That's what everyone's talking about in the barrio. That you're going to lead Little and Big Arroyo in a war of revenge against Smiley's gang. Is that it?"

"So what if it is?"

"Look, be sensible," Mr. West said. "There are other ways."

"Name one."

"The police say that if you cooperate with them . . ."

"Oh, so that's why you're here. The cops sent you," I said.

"No, they didn't send me here, but it's all over the barrio that you didn't tell them who shot Big Toben," Mr. West said.

"I didn't tell them because . . ." my breath became short.

"Because I couldn't."

"I know, I know, the loyalty to your gang code, but what about your family? Your loyalty to your family!" Mr. West said, risking everything.

"I'm gonna do what I have to do," I said as I got up from my father's chair. "If you're finished . . ."

"Yes, I'm through," Mr. West said, standing face-to-face with me. "But I hope you'll think about this long and hard before you do anything that you'll . . ."

"I'll live to regret?"

"Or not live to regret." Mr. West walked out of the house.

In my room, I lay on my bed, thinking.

After awhile I pulled out a shiny, oval mother-of-pearl case from my pocket. When I pushed the silver button buried in the shell, an eight-inch sterling blade flicked out like a snake's tongue. I knew what I had to do.

CHAPTER 15

"Searching"

—The Coasters

After the funeral, I rode home with Speedo, Poison, and Robert. As we drove through the barrio streets, we mumbled curses of revenge for Big Toben's death. We were on watch for any outsiders till dark.

"We'll meet at my house tomorrow," Robert said as I stepped from the '50 Ford to the sidewalk in front of my house.

"Yeah, I'll see you then." I nodded. I put my hands in my pockets and watched the blue Ford roll slowly down the street, out of sight. I walked through my house to the back-yard and stood near the empty pigeon coop.

My fingernails dug into the gray, dried, cracked wood of the coop. I remembered my father's words, "You can learn a lot from the pigeons." I thought about how much I wanted to know. How much I hated Smiley Loco. How much I hated the pain of death, first my father's, now Big Toben's. "Look the world square in the eye," Mr. West had said. What did that mean?

While deep in thought, I had carved a large chunk of wood from the corner of the coop with my fingernails. The old, empty, useless coop made me mad. I got a small hatchet from the back porch and began chopping and hammering at the empty coop with all my strength.

"Firewood, that's all you're good for now!" I began to cry. Soon, my tears and sweat joined with the dry crusty pigeon droppings as the blows scattered pieces of wood and wire in all directions until nothing was left standing. Even though I was very tired, I stacked the largest pieces of wood and bundled the wire mesh in the corner of the yard.

Returning to the bare spot where the coop once stood, I looked up into the dark, empty sky and remembered, "You can learn a lot from the pigeons." I cried out, "The pigeons are gone; my father is gone. How will I ever learn what they have to teach me?" And then all I could think of was the pigeon that carelessly rolled through the air to its death, and Big Toben.

Then I noticed some pigeons gathering on nearby rooftops. With a short flutter of their wings, they landed on top of the wall near me. I recognized my pigeons. Soon twenty or thirty of them crowded on the wall cooing at me.

"Go away," I said. "It's too late. Everything is gone. Everything, see?" I moved both hands out, showing the bare spot where the coop used to be. "Go away, everything, everybody is gone. Go away!"

The pigeons glided down from the wall to land and surround the brown bare spot of earth. They kept at the outer edge of it, until they formed a solid circle of pigeons around it. They cooed, waddled, and strutted in tight circles. But the pigeons wouldn't enter the inner-circle of dirt, as if the bare spot was a hole they could fall into.

"Go away." I stomped the ground near them with my foot. The pigeons stayed. "Go away. It's too late. I don't need you anymore." I kicked my foot out at them, but they barely raised a wing and hopped. "I know what I gotta do. No more questions. All the decisions are made. I don't need your help anymore."

I stamped and kicked my feet as I went toward them, trying to scare them away. But they only parted their huddle as I approached and closed again behind me, like water breaking under a pier. Now I found myself in the center of the bare spot, surrounded by my pigeons, cooing, wing-to-wing, shoulder-to-shoulder.

"I said, go away. Get out of here! I don't want you here!" I felt helpless. I couldn't help my dad, I couldn't help Big Toben and now I couldn't do anything about these pigeons. My eyes swelled with tears. "I'll show you."

Running into the house, I got my BB gun and from the back step, I began shooting at the pigeons. To my surprise, the pigeons stayed, as calm and unafraid as ever alongside their leader, the white pigeon.

"Go away you stupid birds." I began to sob as I heard the gun explode, sending the steel ball straight into the thick gray-feathered bodies of the birds, who flinched with pain, but did not fly away.

"David, what are you doing?" my mother called from inside. I heard her footsteps running toward the back door where I stood.

"Damn you, birds!" I threw the gun down and ran out the back gate into the street. I kept running, past the school, the park, until I reached the narrow dirt road that bordered the drive-in. With my sides aching, and lungs burning, I bent over with my hands on my knees, finally realizing how far I had run without stopping.

When I caught my breath, I walked along the road toward the railroad crossing. When I reached it, the red warning lights started flashing and bells started clanging as the wagging headlight of the train engine came into view. I remembered how many times Robert and I had hopped a slow-moving train just a few blocks for a short ride. Now as the train passed at high speed, I listened to the sing-song clackety-clack of wheels against rails and read the words on the passing freight cars: Chesapeake, Nebraska, Ohio. I began to think how easy it would be to leap at one of the cars, grab hold of the steel ladder, hold on to the narrow shiny rungs until I was far enough away to let go, and never come back.

The sudden calm surprised me when the red caboose passed and left me standing alone as the wig-wag arms went up, letting the traffic pass.

The bright headlights of the oncoming cars made me turn my head away. Then I heard a familiar voice.

"Hey, man," the voice called. "Hey, David."

When I turned to look, I saw Smiley Loco riding in the front seat of his '51 Chevy. As the Chevy pulled up next to me, I put my hand in my back pocket, but the switchblade was gone.

"Hey, man, don't be afraid. Come here. We just wanna talk, man." Smiley Loco looked in the back seat where two of his gang sat, nodding.

Right then, I thought about running. I looked at the well-lit gas station on the corner up ahead and the small grocery store next to it. I knew I would be safe there, but I decided not to run. Instead I moved toward the car, stopping about an arm's length away from Smiley Loco.

"Hey, I heard what you did, man," Smiley Loco looked up at me. "I heard you didn't tell the cops nothing. That's cool, man. It's our fight and we'll settle it between us, eh?" Smiley Loco flashed a sickening grin. "Com'on, man." Smiley extended a skinny-fingered hand for me to shake.

But when Smiley's hand came near, I unloaded a huge lump of spit into his palm. Then Smiley grabbed me by my shirt with his other hand and wiped the spit clean on my chest.

"Look, man," Smiley hissed the words out. "You're just like me. You're no different. You'd like me dead just like Big Toben. There's no difference between you and me and you're going to end up in the same place—no better than me, whether you like it or not."

"No," I said as I punched my ringed fist into Smiley's ugly face, hitting him in the eye and nose hard enough to make blood spurt. When the Chevy's back doors clanked open, I ran down the tracks. But when I looked back, I saw the Chevy following, bouncing along the railroad ties like a drunken beetle. They had to be really angry or crazy to do such a stupid thing I thought as I ran, looking for a way out along the six-foot-high guardrails.

Then a single beam of light came up right ahead of me. There was a slow-moving red and black train engine coming towards me. The hissing of air brakes and flying sparks from the rails let me know that the engineer saw me too. I jumped off the tracks into the cinders, pressing myself tightly against the guardrails. Looking back, I saw the Chevy stop and three doors swing open, letting everyone run out, except Smiley Loco. He was trapped in the back seat. He was tearing at the jacket sleeve that got caught on the door handle. With his other hand he held his nose while little rivers of blood ran between his fingers and down his arm. With its airhorn blearing and brakes locked, the twenty-ton engine slid on metal wheels toward the Chevy. As it neared the car, the bright headlight lit up Smiley's fear-twisted, bleeding face. He screamed when the train struck, plowing the car about a hundred yards down the track before the super chief stopped.

I climbed over the fence, hid in the bushes and watched as the police and emergency teams surrounded the Chevy, crumpled up like a used candy wrapper. They rescued Smiley, who was limp and pale in their hands. The police then rounded up the other gang members, searched and cuffed them. Then I saw a cop, who was searching the trunk, turn and raise a sawed-off shotgun above his head like a door prize.

I found my way along the bushes to the nearest street corner and began walking. Soon a worn, dented old blue pick-up truck stopped near me.

"Where you headed, David?" Mr. García asked as I looked into the cab.

"The cemetery," I blurted out, surprising even myself.

"What?" Mr. García asked.

"I mean, I'm going in that direction to see some friends," I said.

"The cemetery on the hill, right? I'm headed near there. Hop in."

"Thanks, Mr. García." I felt relieved to be with someone I knew.

"You know, I've been thinking about things." Mr. García seemed very serious.

"What about?"

"Your pigeons. You know, the ones you sold to me."

"What about them?" I was afraid he knew that I had shot at them.

I rolled down the window for some fresh air.

"They're always flying over to your place, your backyard." Mr. García looked away from the road ahead and caught my eye. "I think they think they still belong to you."

"Oh, I'm not feeding them or anything," I said. "I really don't know why they come back to me."

"I know you don't, but I've been thinking about this for a while."

"About what?"

"Well, I want you to have them back." Mr. García smiled.

"What? I can't give the money back," I protested. "My mom paid bills with it."

"No, no. I want you to have them." Mr. García made a motion in the air with his hand. "They belong with you. They were always yours."

"But I don't have a coop for them anymore," I whispered, choking back tears.

"I'll help you build another one for them," Mr. García offered as he slowed the truck to a stop. "Here we are."

"Thanks, Mr. García." I got out. "Thanks a lot."

At the cemetery, I paced in front of the ten-foot-high iron gates that were held together with a padlock and chain. Then I climbed over the gates and jumped down to the other side.

I knew I could find my father's grave. I followed the winding paved road that led up a grassy hill scattered with shiny marble gravestones that sparkled in the moonlight.

Underneath a small magnolia, I found my father's grave marker, a polished bronze rectangle, bearing the words "Beloved Father and Husband." As I knelt beside it, I felt the tears hot against my cheeks.

"I need your help. I need to talk to you. I have a lot of questions, but no answers. Help me, Dad, please." I sucked in air and began again. "Big Toben, the pigeons, what should I do?"

While I talked the Santa Ana's swirled around me, keeping me warm. When I put my hand on the gravestone, I remembered something that happened to me a long time ago.

When I was five or six, my father shoved my hand into the crater in my Uncle Julio's leg, a soft, leathery hole where the muscle and skin had been torn away by shrapnel during the war.

"He couldn't take his eyes away from your leg, Julio," my father said, reaching with a calloused hand toward me as I slid back on my butt across the splintery wooden porch, holding my hand as if it had been dropped into boiling water.

"Leave him," Uncle Julio whispered as he sat in cut-off khakis on the front steps, unwinding the string for his kite, "He's my helper, my little kite helper *¿qué no?*"

"*M'ijito*, don't be afraid," Dad said as he stood up, patting me on the head, and looking back at Uncle Julio. "I'm going to work. Are you okay? Do you need anything?"

"I'm okay. The doc says the leg's all right." Uncle Julio's small brown eyes never looked at anyone when he spoke; if he spoke at all. "Like new, he says, like new."

Julio, was a big man, over six-feet-tall and muscular

with wide shoulders, thick arms and a baby face: clean, soft, and round.

"Come here, *m'ijito*," Uncle Julio called to me as he held his arms out, like a priest giving mass, the big yellow kite in one hand and the fat ball of string in the other.

Like all the other days, ever since Uncle Julio was allowed out of bed and the cast had been cut down and molded below his knee, he handed me the back of the kite so that I could grab the sticks where they made a cross. Then I walked backwards, the string slowly unweaving from the stick that he held in his hand. The string ran from the kite along the ground, a winding white line, a nervous squiggle on a page, until he told me to stop.

"Okay, *m'ijo*, when I tell you, you let go of the kite, but wait until I tell you," Uncle Julio said. After wetting his finger in his mouth, he held it high above his head. The breeze would turn it cold. He stared at the distant trees to find the direction of the wind. "Be patient, *m'ijo*."

I held the large, yellow paper kite as high as I could, making sure I wasn't stepping on the tail made from shreds of old bed sheets, knotted together. The kite towered above me and blocked my view of Uncle Julio, but I listened for his signal.

"Now!" Uncle Julio shouted loud enough to scare the dead.

The shout excited me. The string grew stiff. I let go. The great yellow kite zoomed straight into the air like the huge rocket with porthole windows pictured on its front. I watched as Uncle Julio yanked on the string with his big hand like a man ringing a fire bell. The kite answered, flying upward and falling back in a rocking motion, gaining height all the while. Then trouble struck. Caught in cross-winds, the paper kite began spinning counter-clockwise, like a mad bumble bee. Finally, Uncle Julio was able to get it into a place in the sky that held it still, silent as a cloud.

I ran back to the wooden step as Uncle Julio kept working the string from the ball, through his fingers and into the sky; the yellow star was lifting higher into the air. I sat next to Uncle Julio. I watched him ease the tension by letting the string run through his fingers for just an instant before clamping down his thumb again. A game of give-and-take. The kite was rising quickly now. The string dug into the tip of his index finger as he held tightly against the pain. The kite flew above us like a winged phantom. Then he dropped the spool of string, leaving it spinning on the dirt in front of us. The kite wanted to get away. Uncle Julio held the string tightly with both hands, knowing it had to be held until it found its own way.

I looked down at Uncle Julio's dull white cast covered with friends' writings and cartoon drawings, like Mickey Mouse, which Uncle Julio had drawn himself. I wondered if it hurt, but whenever I asked, no one ever answered me, except once.

"Mom, does Uncle Julio's leg hurt him?" I asked when she was fixing dinner in the kitchen. She stopped stirring the beans and dried her hands on her apron as she knelt down to talk to me.

"Shhhh, don't ask anymore, okay?" She put her arm around me. "It's not the hurt here." She touched my leg. "It's the hurt here that won't go away." She put her fingers to my heart. "So don't ask anymore, okay?"

Uncle Julio kept looking upward as he let go of yards and yards of string as the kite caught the wind, sailed into the sky, and disappeared from sight.

"Pretty soon we'll need more string," Uncle Julio would remind me as he sat there on the front doorstep all day just flying his kite. I sat with him, quietly looking at the sky, sometimes the clouds rolled by in herds or in single file, like buffalo.

As I watched, I remembered what my father explained once, that Uncle Julio often thought about his dead friend, the one who saved his life by jumping on top of the grenade that blew his head off and sent a piece of metal, large as a baseball into Uncle Julio's thigh, knocking him down and unconscious.

At noon, my mother set a plate with warm, folded flour tortillas and beans next to Uncle Julio, who said nothing as he wedged the stick of string, almost gone, into the empty space between the steps, freeing his hands to eat.

"Do you want to hold it?" He teased me, knowing that once before I had asked to hold it, only to grab hold of the stick of string and have it ripped away by the sudden tug of the kite. We watched as the kite wobbled in the sky and the ball of string slid along the ground until it got tangled in a hedge.

"Step on it with your foot."

I stamped my foot down. Then grabbed the string with both hands and brought it back to Uncle Julio.

"There's only one way to lose a kite, and that's to let it go." He grinned at me, his white teeth showing.

By late afternoon I had been sent to the corner store to get three balls of string to add to the supply. Now the kite, a faint yellow diamond in the sky, pulled on the string as it grew from Uncle Julio's hand like a bean stalk, burning a crease deeper into his finger. Our eyes followed the line of string, bowing under its own weight, held in the sky as if by magic, always lengthening, as it slipped through Uncle Julio's fingers.

Usually at about dusk, Uncle Julio would begin to bring in the kite with a steady figure-eight weaving of the string around the stick as he guided the kite down, but today was different. Instead of bringing the kite in, he pressed another dime into my hand, signaling me to go and get another ball of string. I hesitated. Uncle Julio urged me on with a stern look.

When I returned with the new supply, Uncle Julio tied it to the last bit of string left on the stick and slowly let it out. He watched the string stretch out into the sky while the kite disappeared completely from sight. Then Uncle Julio managed to stand up without his crutches and hold the stick above his head, with the last bit of new string tied to it.

I heard him whisper something as he slipped the knotted string from the stick, freeing the kite into the air. We watched the end of the string wriggle into the sky as it played over treetops tangling and untangling, then lifting into the dusk, disappearing altogether.

I turned to Uncle Julio for some kind of explanation, but he offered none. He only rubbed his moist eyes with his knuckles before he led me inside.

The next morning my mother shook me awake and asked me to say good-bye to Uncle Julio. I ran to the front doorstep.

"Here *m'ijo*, here's a present for you." Uncle Julio managed a smile.

I took the piece of paper from his hand and began to cry at the same time.

"Good-bye."

I heard the words between the adults as I watched Uncle Julio get into my father's brown Chevy and drive away. In my hand was Uncle Julio's gift, a neat pencil drawing of a rocket, fire blasting from its engines, shooting into the sky forever.

When the memory ended, I found myself back at my father's grave, lifting my closed hand toward the darkened sky and then opening it slowly until all my fingers were open and free.

In my mind, I saw a fast frame replay of my life—my father's empty chair; the pigeons flying, falling; my mother crying; my Uncle Joe pointing a finger at me; Big Toben's hands pushing at my chest; Mr. West crossing his arms; Miss Johnson standing tall, guarding; Robert closing his eyes, holding his head down; Smiley reaching for a handshake; and Mr. García at the wheel of his pick-up.

With tears running down my face, I knelt beside my father's grave, and spoke, "Mother was right. An eye for an eye has to stop. On Big Toben's gravemarker it said only "Beloved Son" and that was all. His mother was the last to leave his grave, just as my grandmother was the last to leave my dad's. I don't want my mother to suffer like that for me."

CHAPTER 16

At home I woke to the sound of my mother in the kitchen rattling pots and pans, a sure sign for me to get up. On the table I found a glass of milk and, leaning against it, an envelope addressed to me. Around the table sat Henry, Rosie, Barbara, and Susie wide-eyed, staring. Mother must have told them something, I thought.

"It came in the mail yesterday," said Mom.

"Open it. Open it," the girls urged, while Henry sat smiling quietly.

"Hey, wait a minute." I played with their excitement. "I'm not going on TV or anything like Rosie did."

"Hurry, open it," Rosie said.

I looked at the envelope carefully, seeing the return address: "Stanford Scholarship Essay Contest." I opened the envelope by wedging my finger under the sealed flap.

Inside I found a one page letter that read: "Congratulations! Your essay, 'Las Palomas, My Homing Pigeons,' has been awarded first prize by our distinguished panel of judges. You will receive a $500 scholarship upon entrance to an accredited high school and an opportunity to receive additional scholarships throughout your high school and college careers."

"Mom, I won a scholarship," I said and slumped in my chair, limp as a sack of beans.

"What? Let's see." She read the letter as tears formed in the corners of her green eyes. "David, this is wonderful. *¡Qué milagro!*"

"Gee, David, you're so smart." Rosie stood up from her chair and hugged me. The others gathered around me in a tight cluster.

"I want you to see something else," Mom said. She walked to the kitchen and returned with a large brown paper bag. "Look inside."

I slowly undid the worn opening and looked inside.

"Where did all this money come from?" I stared into the bag. My brother and sisters squealed with excitement.

"Mr. García brought it to us. It's from the neighbors. They want us to have it. It's a 'gift of love' they said." My mother began to cry.

"I can't believe it."

"It's true. It's true. We need to thank everyone." Mom gathered us around her.

"I know. I need to talk to Robert," I said as I headed to the front door. "I'll be right back."

Once inside Robert's house, I went to his bedroom.

"I'm going to see Miss Johnson," I said, watching Robert who was bent over, looking into the dresser mirror. "Are you coming?"

"What for?" replied Robert, combing back his hair as

he turned to face me. "I don't have anything to say to her."

"Okay, okay, but I'm going to see her." I gripped the bedpost.

"What about, Eastside?" Robert stood in front of me. "Speedo wants to get together, Little and Big Arroyo, to get Eastside, Smiley Loco, for what they did."

"I don't know."

"What? What are you saying?" Robert paced.

"I can't. Not now."

"What the hell are you talking about? Big Toben's dead," Robert tugged at his shirt. "We can't let them get away with that!"

"Listen to me, Robert. The cops got Smiley Loco last night. I told you that!"

"He'll be out in no time." Robert circled, then aimed. "You're chicken!"

"Think what you want! You fight your way, I'll fight mine!" I pounded my fist against my chest. "There's got to be another way."

"You're chicken!"

"We've always done it this way. Where does it get us? Go ahead, join Big Arroyo and Speedo. See what it gets you." I swallowed. "Maybe dead, that's all!"

"You coming with us, or not?"

"No! I'm outta here!"

"You chicken shit!" Robert strode out of the room, through the front door where Speedo was waiting in his car parked in the street, leaving me standing in the doorway, watching.

At school, before anyone else arrived, I saw Miss Johnson sitting at her desk, reading a book as streams of light flowed through the window blinds.

"Here, sit here," she said, waving for me to sit at a desk near her. I walked slowly, then sank into the chair. My eyes looked down. My hands were clasped together on top of the desk.

"There's talk of revenge for Danny's, that is, Big Toben's death." Miss Johnson looked at me over her opened book. "Is that true?"

"No. I mean yes. Some of the guys want revenge," I said, my hand rubbing my forehead.

"I know it must be difficult for you," said Miss Johnson. "Did you receive a letter from Stanford? Here's the copy the Principal gave me."

"Yes, I got it, and well, Miss Johnson, I want you to know that I'm sorry for causing trouble in your class, and, well, thanks for your help. I really mean that." I let the words run out in one big breath, afraid that it wouldn't get said at all.

"I know. I, I think sometimes it's just hard to tell someone . . ."

As I listened to her speak, I looked out the window and saw the pigeons outside, soaring, wings outspread, tilting and turning, cutting invisible paths in the air, and showing me what I had to do, and which way I had to go.